"The shop's not open," Melinda called from behind the counter.

"Your door is." Daniel's boots tramped across the wood floor until his long, jean-clad legs materialized in front of the display case. "Hey, Goldilocks. Looks like you're hard at work."

"I am." Melinda considered asking him if he'd enjoyed his date with April, but thought better of it. Instead, she squirted window cleaner on the next section of glass.

"Is Aunt Martha planning to reopen the shop?"

"We're thinking about it." She swirled the glass cleaner around, blurring her view of his legs.

"That a fact?" he drawled, an arrogant grin in his voice. "Want some help?"

She lifted her head too fast, whacking it on the inside of the display case. She rubbed the back of her skull.

"No! I'm fine." She looked up at him. Foolish woman! She should've known he'd be grinning at her, a grin that crinkled the corners of his eyes and made his dark eyes flash with amusement.

Books by Charlotte Carter

Love Inspired

Montana Hearts
Big Sky Reunion

CHARLOTTE CARTER

A multipublished author of more than fifty romances, cozy mysteries and inspirational titles, Charlotte Carter lives in Southern California with her husband of forty-nine years and their cat, Mittens. They have two married daughters and five grandchildren. When she's not writing, Charlotte does a little stand-up comedy, "G-Rated Humor for Grownups," and teaches workshops on the craft of writing.

Big Sky Reunion
Charlotte Carter

Love Inspired

Recycling programs
for this product may
not exist in your area.

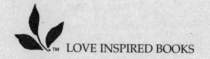 LOVE INSPIRED BOOKS

ISBN-13: 978-0-373-87670-9

BIG SKY REUNION

www.LoveInspiredBooks.com

Printed in U.S.A.

Blessed are those whose transgressions are forgiven,
whose sins are covered.
Blessed is the one whose sin the Lord
will never count against them.
—*Romans* 4:7, 8

Special thanks to Nancy Farrier
for sharing her knowledge of the inspirational
market, helping me with the plot and
for simply being a really nice person.

Chapter One

"Hey, look who's back in town. Goldilocks."

Melinda Spencer whirled. Shock slammed into her like a runaway truck. Her eyes widened and she took a step back.

Gazing down at her was the original bad boy of Potter Creek, Montana. His dark eyes held the same teasing glint she remembered from ten years ago. His easy slouch and the cocky way his Stetson sat tipped back on his head suggested he hadn't changed one whit since she last saw him.

Since the day she'd gotten on a bus to hightail her way out of Montana and back to her home in Pittsburgh. She'd lost her heart to this dark-eyed Romeo.

She narrowed her eyes and folded her arms across her chest. "Hello, Daniel. I thought you'd be long gone from here by now." Probably in jail or killed in a bar fight.

One corner of his mouth kicked up a notch. "Nope. This is my hometown. I'm here to stay."

"Good for you," she said, deadpan. She turned her back on him to finish the task he'd interrupted, unlocking the door to Aunt Martha's Knitting and Notions shop. The silly key didn't want to work, which had nothing to do with her fingers that had suddenly turned clumsy.

"What brings you to town?" Daniel asked.

She went still for a moment, then looked over her shoulder. "Aunt Martha had a stroke. I brought her home from the rehab facility this morning. I'm here to take care of her."

"So you're not planning to stay long?"

"I'll stay as long as she needs me." In truth, she didn't have much of anywhere else to go, but she wasn't going to tell Daniel O'Brien that.

She resumed her efforts with the obstinate key.

"Here, let me help you."

He reached around her, his hand closing over hers, his fingers long and deeply tanned. His forearm had a light covering of dark hair over corded muscles. He was too close, so close she caught the scent of the prairie on his shirt and the unique masculine aroma that was his alone.

Memories of being seventeen years old and foolish assailed her. Memories she'd never been able to completely bury even when she'd married another boy, the one who had taken her to the senior prom.

She yanked her hand away, her heart thudding like the hooves of a quarter horse galloping across the open landscape.

The lock released its grip on the door. Daniel shoved it open.

"There you go, Goldilocks. Welcome to Aunt Martha's Knitting and Notions." With a mock bow, he gestured for her to enter the small shop.

Instead she held out her hand. "The key."

His eyes twinkling, his lips curved upward, he dropped it in her hand.

"Thank you." She stepped inside, intending to close the door behind her, leaving him standing on the cracked sidewalk that ran the length of Main Street.

No such luck.

Like a predator on the prowl, he slipped past her and sauntered into the store.

Bins for yarn lined two walls from floor to ceiling, but many were empty. Other bins were a jumble, worsteds mixed with baby weight yarn, variegated and solid colors randomly mingled in the same bin. The display rack for knitting needles, crochet hooks, stitch markers and other notions canted at a precarious angle and the pattern books tucked into a pocket display looked as though they'd been published in the 1950s.

In a back corner of the room sat a table and six unmatched dining room chairs that had been used for knitting classes. Odds and ends of yarn were scattered about the table.

Daniel picked up a skein of merino yarn and tossed it gently in the air, catching it and tossing it again as a young boy might toss a baseball. In no way, however, did Daniel O'Brien resemble anything other than a full-grown cowboy with an attitude.

"It smells musty in here. Better leave the door open and air out the place." He tossed the skein back in the bin where he'd found it.

Melinda wrinkled her nose. "I don't think that Aunt Martha has opened the store in weeks." Martha, even at age eighty-two, had always been lively and energetic, busy in the community and with her church work, until the stroke felled her. Or so Melinda had thought.

From the disarray in the shop and out-of-date stock, she suspected her great-aunt hadn't spent a lot of time serving her customers in recent years. Assuming she had any customers left.

Her shoulders sank. Not only had she planned to help her aunt during her recovery, but she'd also desperately hoped to turn Aunt Martha's Knitting and Notions into a profitable business that would support them both.

Apparently God didn't care what she wanted. Not that she deserved His help.

Still skulking around and poking into things, Daniel said, "I heard you got married a while back. Your husband come to town with you?"

Despite the ten-inch needle of grief that stabbed her in the chest, she lifted her chin. "I'm widowed."

That stopped him in his tracks. The teasing glint vanished from his eyes and his brows tugged together. "I'm sorry. I hadn't heard that." He lifted his Stetson, ran his fingers through his thick, dark hair and resettled his hat. "You got kids?"

"No." No husband. No child—not anymore. She'd as much as killed them both with her own hand. Her chin quivered. She bit down on her lip, turned away and walked behind the counter to the ancient cash register.

"If you don't mind, I'd like to check the inventory and some of Aunt Martha's records." She looked at him expectantly, willing him to leave.

He straightened to his full six feet two. "You want me to get lost."

"Yes, please." Her teeth clenched.

He shrugged, an easy roll of broad shoulders beneath a blue work shirt that pulled tautly across his chest. He'd filled out in the past ten years and looked as though he was used to hard work. Which, remembering his wildness, the way he'd loved to party and drive at reckless speeds, was hard for her to believe.

"Then I'll catch you later, Goldilocks." He winked and ambled to the door.

She watched him walk down the sidewalk past the shop's dusty display window, all loose limbs and easy gate. His buddies used to call him Swagger.

He called her Goldilocks.

"My name is Melinda," she whispered to herself. Goldilocks and her wide-eyed innocence no longer existed. That foolish person had endured a painful death along with her son, Jason.

Daniel still had that arrogant swagger that had hooked her the moment he'd walked across Riverside Park to stand two feet in front of her. In a low, husky voice, he'd said, "Hi, Goldilocks. Wanna go for a ride in my truck?"

To her dismay, a part of her still did.

* * *

Daniel reached his pickup parked a few doors down from Martha's shop. He'd driven into town to pick up a prescription from the pharmacy. When he'd spotted Goldilocks, he'd been so surprised that a dust devil racing across the prairie could've blown him over.

Opening the truck door, he smiled to himself. He would've recognized her golden curls from a mile away. Long and bouncy and woven of pure silk.

A city girl, she'd been sent out west to spend the summer with her great-aunt Martha before her final year of high school. Daniel had spotted her right off then, too. Even knowing she was too young and he ought to keep his distance, he'd been drawn to her like a horse to a quartered apple in his hand.

He'd teased and cajoled and lured her with every bit of charm he had.

But Miss Goody Two-Shoes had won out. She told him no and skedaddled back home to Pittsburgh without so much as a wave goodbye.

That hadn't done his ego a bit of good. Not that his ego hadn't needed a good kick in the butt back then.

She was different now. Older. Maybe wiser. A widow with a hint of sadness shadowing her baby-blue eyes. No longer a girl, now she was a full-grown woman.

But she hadn't given him a single sign that Goldilocks had any interest in a second time around.

He climbed into the cab of the extended pickup, which was baking hot from sitting out in the summer sun.

He wondered how long she'd stay in Potter Creek

this time. Long enough for him to get a second chance to prove he wasn't a worthless cowboy?

Sweat crept down his back and he licked his lips. It might be worth a shot—if she stuck around for a while.

The O'Brien ranch lay a little northwest of Potter Creek, less than thirty minutes away. Daniel and his older brother, Arnie, ran a hundred head of beef cattle on the place and Daniel pursued his passion for breeding quarter horses. His mares had foaled some of the top-ranked quarter horses in the state and he got big bucks for his stallions to service mares owned by other horse owners.

Turning off the highway, he drove under the wrought-iron arch at the entrance to O'Brien Ranch and bumped over the cattle guard. The driveway bordered the horse pasture on the right and led to a two-story white house his grandfather had built.

A house and ranch his father had nearly destroyed in a drunken haze that lasted around fifty years, until his death.

April, his favorite sorrel mare, trotted over to the fence. He tooted his horn and she shook her blond mane in response, keeping pace with the truck until she reached the end of the pasture.

He pulled the truck up next to the barn and parked just as Arnie came out of the open double doors riding his shiny red ATV.

"Yo, bro." Daniel swung down from the truck. "What's happening?"

Using hand controls, Arnie brought the ATV to a

halt. His dog, Sheila, a golden retriever mix, sat proudly behind him. "What I want to know is what took you so long, Danny boy. Had Doc Harper gone fishing?"

Daniel slapped himself on the forehead. Doc Harper was the town pharmacist. "The prescription. I forgot to pick it up."

Arnie gave him a steady-eyed look and slowly raised his brows. Although they both had inherited their mother's olive complexion and the telltale cheekbones of the Blackfoot Indians, Arnie's upper body was more muscular than Daniel's. His legs, though, had withered considerably since the accident that had paralyzed him eight years ago.

"You got distracted, I gather," he said.

"Yep, you could say that."

"Good lookin'?"

Heat from more than the sun flooded Daniel's cheeks. "Mindy Spencer's back in town." He used the nickname for Melinda that family and close friends used. "She's helping her aunt."

Arnie's eyes widened and he tilted his head. "If Ivy hears about Mindy, she might not be too happy."

Scowling, Daniel shook his head. "Ivy doesn't have any claim on me."

"She'd sure like to." Taking off his hat, Arnie wiped the sweat from the inside of the hat band. "Is Mindy planning to stay permanently?"

"She said not."

"Interesting." Arnie shifted the ATV into gear. "Have a nice ride back to town."

Daniel held out his hands, palms up. "Ah, come

on, Arnie. The prescription can wait till tomorrow, can't it?"

"Tomorrow's Sunday. Doc Harper closes up shop on Sundays." He drove the ATV to the back porch of the house. Sheila agilely jumped down and waited while Arnie unloaded the wheelchair from the back of the all-terrain vehicle. Using a trapeze device Daniel had jerry-rigged for him, Arnie lifted himself out of the ATV and into the chair. "Say hello to Mindy for me next time you see her."

Daniel jammed his hands in his pockets. "Yeah. Right."

Chortling a big-brother laugh that put Daniel's teeth on edge, Arnie wheeled himself up the ramp and into the house, Sheila right behind him, ready to be of service whenever she was needed.

Yanking open the truck door, Daniel got inside. He'd go into town. Get the prescription. And come right back. Like he was supposed to have done the first time.

Unless Goldilocks was still hanging around the knitting shop.

Then he might stick around for a while.

Chapter Two

Head down, her footsteps as slow as a desert tortoise, Melinda left Knitting and Notions to walk the short distance to Aunt Martha's house.

She hadn't spent long in the shop after Daniel left. Realizing how much needed to be done to get the store up and running was a daunting prospect. First, a top-to-bottom cleaning would be needed, followed by re-arranging the stock and ordering new yarns and notions. Advertisements would have to be created and placed in the local biweekly newspaper, flyers made and posted around town about classes and special activities.

To make the shop a profitable venture, she'd have to attract customers not only from Potter Creek and its five thousand residents, but from the surrounding area, as well. Which meant she'd be competing with shops in Bozeman, less than an hour away.

Daunting was an understatement.

For as long as Melinda could remember, Martha had lived in a small one-story stucco house facing Second

Street, directly behind the shop. The large backyard used to be a riot of color during the summer, roses in full bloom, morning glories scampering up a trellis, beds of purple iris and lilac bushes. Ten years ago Melinda had helped her aunt put up jars and jars of vegetables she'd grown in her garden, most of which she'd given to the church's food pantry to help the poor.

Now the yard had gone scraggly and overgrown. Only the indestructible morning glories struggled onward and upward, covering the trellis with bright blue flowers.

The house looked as ragged as the yard with its chipped paint and dangling window screens.

Guilt punched a hole in Melinda's chest. A knot tightened in her stomach. So much had changed in the past ten years. She should have kept better track of her aunt's situation instead of focusing only on her own problems.

For three agonizing years, she'd devoted her life, day and night, to Jason. The last two she'd rarely left his side or thought of anything but his well-being.

The steps wobbled as she walked up onto the porch where a wicker slider sat, dusty and abandoned.

In the kitchen, which featured a circa-1950 chrome-and-Formica table and a white tile counter, the dishes she'd washed after their lunch sat drying on the drain board. From the living room, she heard the sound of the TV playing.

Aunt Martha sat in her favorite wingback chair, the remote control in her hand, her walker right next to her chair. Her collapsible wheelchair was in the front entry if she needed it.

"Hello, Mindy, dear. Did you pick out some yarn while you were in the shop?" Due to the stroke, the right side of Martha's mouth didn't work quite right and her speech was slightly slurred. Her hair had long since gone from the blond of her youth to silver-gray, and her face was lined from a lifetime of Montana sunshine and hours of hearty laughter.

"Not today. I brought along a sweater I've been meaning to finish for ages. I'll work on that first." She picked up the newspaper Martha had dropped on the floor and set it on the coffee table. "Anything I can get for you?"

"No, I'm fine. I don't want you to trouble yourself over me."

"That's why I'm here, Aunt Martha. Have you done your afternoon exercises yet?"

"Oh, pshaw, child. Those therapists at Manhattan Rehab purely wore me out. I'm taking today off."

Frowning, Melinda picked up the rubber ball her aunt was supposed to squeeze multiple times during the day and handed it to Martha. "You aren't going to be able to knit a stitch if you don't get your strength back in your hands."

Martha looked up over the top of her glasses at Melinda. "You've turned into a bossy little thing, haven't you, child?" With a funny twist of her lips, and considerable effort, she held out her hand for the ball.

Melinda placed it in her palm. "Now squeeze."

Martha did as instructed.

Sitting down in the floral-print love seat, Melinda stretched out her legs. She wiggled her toes in her sandals. She wasn't wearing polish on her toenails and idly wondered if Daniel had noticed.

Rejecting the thought, she sat up straighter, pulling her feet closer to the sofa.

"Before your stroke, were you still teaching knitting classes?"

"Oh, my goodness, no, dear. Young people don't seem so interested in knitting these days and most of the ladies who used to come into the shop have either died or moved into an old folks' home in Bozeman or Manhattan. Unless someone called for something special, I've hardly opened the door for the past year or so."

Which explained both the obstinate key and the disarray in the shop. Melinda puffed out her cheeks on a long exhale.

"I was thinking… I thought I might reopen the shop." She chose her words carefully. Her heart stuttered in the same uncertain rhythm. "Maybe stay in Potter Creek permanently."

Eyes widening and a lopsided smile creasing her cheeks, Martha said, "That would be so nice, dear, but are you sure you want to be stuck in a small town like Potter Creek? There isn't much for young people to do here."

Then why had Daniel stuck around?

"You remember, I was managing a knitting and needlework store until—" her voice broke and she struggled to keep a tremor from her lips "—until Jason got so sick."

"That poor little boy. I was so sorry—"

"The shop built up a really nice clientele," she hurried on, unwilling and unable to talk about her son. "Mostly women, of course, but quite a few young mothers. Even some teenagers. The classes were filled all of the time and we kept adding new ones."

Moving her right arm awkwardly, Martha put the rubber ball in her lap. "Is that what you'd like to do with my shop?"

"After your hospital social worker called me about your discharge plan, I got to thinking about the shop and how much you'd taught me that summer I visited. I wouldn't do anything with the shop without your approval." She did need to keep busy, though. She couldn't go on wallowing in self-pity and isolating herself from human contact as she had for the past six months.

Using her left hand, Martha lifted her right hand and brought them both to her chest. "Praise the Lord! I've been praying He'd give me a sign of what I should do. Now God has answered my prayer and sent you to me."

Slanting her gaze to the worn and faded Oriental carpet on the floor, Melinda shook her head. "I don't think I'm God's answer to anything. But I do need to work, Aunt Martha." Regret and grief nearly choking her, she lifted her head. "I'm broke. I had to declare bankruptcy last month." Enormous medical bills had taken every dime she'd received after her husband's death—a death benefit from the defense contractor who'd employed him as a civilian truck driver in Afghanistan. An IED had blown up under his vehicle. Even then, she'd still owed thousands of dollars for Jason's care. She'd had no choice but to file for bankruptcy and start over again.

Alone.

Desperately trying to stitch her life back together again.

"I'm so sorry, Mindy. If I'd known…"

She tried to shrug off her aunt's sympathy, but it felt like ice picks were being jammed into her spine one after the other, cutting off the messages from her brain to her muscles. The pain paralyzed her.

"Of course you can run the shop, dear. I won't be of much help, but I'm sure you have some wonderful ideas."

The tension drained from her shoulders. The tightness she'd been holding in eased and her facial muscles relaxed.

She had a job and a task that was so daunting she wouldn't be able to think of the past. Maybe she'd even be able to sleep at night without the dreams that had haunted her for the past three years.

One problem remained. Now that she was going to stay, what was she going to do about Daniel and the feelings she had for him that had never quite gone away?

Foolish feelings she should have discarded when she put on Joe's wedding ring.

* * *

After dinner, Melinda decided to finish her unpacking. She'd brought only two suitcases with her. Her few other possessions she'd stored with a friend to be shipped later—if she decided to stay in Potter Creek.

She'd stayed in Aunt Martha's guest room ten years ago, the narrow twin bed and varnished pine bedside table and matching dresser familiar to her.

Shaking out her clothes, she hung them in the small walk-in closet: casual blouses and slacks, the ubiquitous jeans that was the uniform in small Montana towns. A few pairs of shorts and tank tops for the scorching days of summer.

At the bottom of the suitcase she found her Bible. Sitting on the edge of the bed, she held it for a moment and rubbed her fingertip over the faux-leather cover. For years she'd read the Bible or a book of daily devotions every morning. And she'd prayed.

But no longer.

Tears sprang to her eyes, blurring her vision. Her chin quivered. The bitter taste of failure, of God's censure, filled her throat. He would never forgive her. Nor could she forgive herself.

She opened the drawer in the bedside table and tossed the Bible inside where it would be out of sight, no longer a reminder of lost hope.

As the Bible landed with a thump, the cover flew open. A snapshot slid out.

She covered her mouth with her hand to prevent a sob. Jason. Two years old. A towhead with a beatific smile, wearing his swimsuit, running through the sprinklers on a hot afternoon. A perfect child. As smart and quick as an Olympic athlete and just learning to talk. She could still hear him calling her.

"Mommy! Mommy! Watch me! Watch me!"

Tears rolled down Melinda's cheeks unabated. In three short years he'd gone from that beautiful child to little more than skin and bones, racked with pain with every breath he took, unable to walk or talk.

A sense of panic, of not being able to breathe, started like a coiling snake in her midsection. Twisting and turning and spinning, a tornado of blackness rose into her throat. Her head threatened to explode. Muscles and bones lacked strength and began to crumble. She was falling, falling…

Brain tumor. No hope. Vegetative state.

"I'm so sorry, baby. So sorry." She slid off the bed onto the floor and buried her face in her hands. "I'm so sorry."

A counselor had told Melinda she'd effectively been in a war zone for three full years struggling to save her child. She was suffering from PTSD, post-traumatic stress disorder.

Knowing hadn't changed a thing.

God hadn't saved her baby boy.

The following morning, Aunt Martha insisted they go to church.

Melinda tried to talk her out of it. "You're not strong enough yet."

"Nonsense, child. I can sit in church as well as I

can sit at home. And I need to thank the good Lord for saving my life and bringing you to stay with me."

Clearly she could do her thanking right here in the living room, but it was impossible to argue with Aunt Martha.

No matter that she was sweet and syrupy and full of lopsided smiles, she wasn't about to give an inch.

No matter that Melinda didn't belong in any church.

So, with her teeth clamped tightly together and her jaw aching, Melinda wheeled her aunt out to her fifteen-year-old Buick sedan, helped her into the car and drove her to church.

And, of course, she couldn't simply drop her aunt off and come back in an hour, although that's exactly what Melinda would have preferred. Instead she had to help her into her wheelchair and push her up the walkway to the double-door entrance of Potter Creek Community Church.

The whitewashed structure wasn't the largest church in town, but it did have the tallest steeple. Today, instead of beckoning her inside, it seemed to cast a shadow over Melinda that said she wasn't welcome. She kept her head down and her arms close to her body as she pushed her aunt into the cool interior.

"Morning, Aunt Martha," a familiar masculine voice said. "Glad you're back home and out on the town."

Melinda stopped stark still and her head snapped up. Daniel O'Brien? At church? Dressed in a fine-cotton Western-style shirt and slacks? Greeting folks as they arrived?

She blinked and shook her head. She must be hallucinating. The Daniel O'Brien she remembered wouldn't have been caught dead in church on Sunday morning or any other time.

A smile curved his lips and crinkled the corners of his eyes. "Good to see you, too, Mindy." His dark brows lifted ever so slightly as he handed Aunt Martha and Melinda each a program for the morning service.

Melinda wanted to take it and run. Instead she gave him a curt nod and pushed her aunt past Daniel as quickly as she could. They didn't get far. Several of Martha's longtime friends spotted her. They gathered around, most of them as gray-haired as her aunt, welcoming her back home. A few looked vaguely familiar to Melinda, but she couldn't recall their names.

"We've been so worried about you."

"The prayer circle has been praying for you."

"Isn't it nice your niece could come stay with you for a bit."

Melinda forced a smile that instantly froze on her face. She was annoyingly aware of Daniel standing no more than five feet behind her. In his deep baritone voice, he greeted new arrivals, all of whom he knew by name. They responded with the same warmth of friendship that he had extended.

She felt like Alice slipping down the rabbit hole and discovering Daniel was the king of hearts.

Where had his wild side gone? The risk taker who drove a hundred miles per hour down the highway. The fighter who'd landed in the town jail more than once. The daredevil who raced a train to the crossing—and won. Barely. Leaving her breathless that they had escaped death and releasing her own wild side that she'd never known lurked somewhere inside her.

Did his new persona merely mask the man who had kissed her so thoroughly and wanted more? He would have gotten it, too, if Aunt Martha hadn't returned home earlier than expected.

Heat flamed Melinda's face as she remembered that memorable August evening ten years ago. She'd left town the next day right after an older girl, DeeDee Pickens, had flaunted the ring Daniel had given her.

"Hope you know you don't stand a chance with my Danny boy," DeeDee had crowed.

Melinda parked Martha's chair at the end of a pew near the back of the church and slipped past her to take a seat.

Reverend Arthur Redmond, the pastor according to the program, looked to be in his early fifties and graying at the temples. His voice carried to the back of the room with ease as he welcomed the congregation to his church.

Melinda lowered her gaze, pretending to study the program. Tears blurred her vision. No matter what the pastor said, she knew her sins were too great to be forgiven.

The service seemed excruciatingly long. She sat with her eyes cast downward, her hands clasped tightly in her lap, knowing she didn't belong in church. Wishing she could flee back to the knitting shop to scrub it clean and start over, in the same way she'd start a new knitting project with clean needles and a fresh skein of yarn.

Finally Reverend Redmond released his grip on the congregation and allowed them to file out into the warm sun. As though she'd been released from prison, Melinda drew in a deep breath of fresh air tinged with the scent of sage.

"Pastor Redmond surely knows how to preach, doesn't he?" Martha said. "I feel renewed every time I hear his sermons."

Melinda didn't respond. She'd spotted Daniel off to the side of the parking area shooting baskets with a half-dozen high school boys. It appeared to be a two-on-six game as he agilely dribbled past two boys, sank a banked shot, then stole the ball back from another youngster. He flipped the ball to a man in a wheelchair, who neatly made a lay-up shot.

Her forehead furrowed and she squinted. Could that be Daniel's brother, Arnie?

She dragged her gaze away and pushed her aunt's wheelchair toward the car. After settling Aunt Martha in the front seat, Melinda walked around to the driver's side. She took one last look at the basketball game.

A young woman, probably in her twenties, wearing heels and a floral-print dress, went tiptoeing out onto the basketball court and snatched the ball away from Daniel.

"Hey!" he complained, trying to grab it back.

The brunette scooted toward the basket without bothering to dribble the ball. "What's the matter, Danny? Don't you let girls play in your league?"

The teenage boys hooted and hollered. A couple of

teenage girls, who'd been preening as they watched the game, shouted, "Way to go, Ivy."

Standing with his legs wide apart, hands on his hips, Daniel watched the young woman with an amused smile on his lips.

She launched the ball underhanded toward the hoop. It fell well short and one of the teenagers snagged it on the bounce.

"Oh, well." The brunette cocked her hip toward Daniel and gave him a long, leisurely smile. "You coming in for the Sunday special, Danny?"

He intercepted a pass between two teenagers. "Nope, I've got a date with April."

Melinda chose not to watch any longer. Daniel hadn't changed. He still had an eye for the women, and they reciprocated the feeling.

Which was of no concern to her.

As she backed the Buick out of its parking spot, she said, "I was surprised to see Daniel O'Brien at church."

"Oh, yes, when he was a youngster he was a bit wild, but he's become a fine young man. Not at all like his no-account father, God rest his soul. Daniel's taken an interest in the church youth group."

Probably to lead them astray, Melinda thought uncharitably. "Was that his brother in the wheelchair?" Arnie had been the solid, responsible older brother. So far as Melinda knew, he'd never gotten into trouble or broken any laws. Daniel had had almost as many battles with his brother as he had with his father.

"Yes, that was Arnie. Poor boy. Had a terrible

accident a few years back." Martha pulled a hankie from her purse and dabbed at the perspiration on her face and neck. "Can't remember just how long ago. It left him paralyzed from his waist down. The past few years, those two boys have been nearly inseparable."

There Melinda went, sliding down the rabbit hole again.

The whole world had slipped off-kilter since she'd seen Daniel at church.

That wasn't an image she'd ever had of him. She couldn't believe what she'd seen and learned about him. It had to be an act, all smoke and mirrors.

A wolf couldn't change his killer instincts.

Daniel couldn't change his instincts, either. Beneath the charade, he was still Potter Creek's baddest of bad boys.

He had to be.

Back at the ranch, Daniel made himself a roast beef sandwich with mustard and lettuce, and washed it down with a soda. In the upcoming Potato Festival in Manhattan, he and April, his best cutting horse, were entered in the cow-cutting and trail-riding events. Last year Charlie Moffett from Three Forks had beaten him in both events, Daniel's first loss in six years.

Charlie had lorded it over him for nearly a year.

Daniel took a big bite of his sandwich and chewed down hard. That wasn't going to happen again. The reputation of the quarter horses he raised and trained was at stake. Not to mention the income they produced for O'Brien Ranch.

The double prize money when he won both events would punch up the bank account so they could pay the balloon installment on this year's mortgage bill, a result of refinancing the ranch to modernize the place seven years ago.

Outside the afternoon had heated up. In the distance, dark clouds had begun to form over the mountains. They wouldn't amount to much this time of year. Along about August they'd bring some much-needed rain, even a few gully washers, and plenty of thunder and lightning. Maybe even start a wildfire or two.

In the shade of the barn, Daniel saddled April. A sorrel with a blond mane and tail, she was a sturdy girl with strong legs and a sweet disposition.

"You're a sweetheart, aren't you, love." He tightened the cinch under her belly and checked the stirrups. "This time we'll leave Charlie and his swayback nag in the dust. He'll stop his crowing on his Facebook page. Best Quarter Horse Breeder in Montana, my foot."

Arnie and his dog, Sheila, arrived at the corral on his ATV. "You're sure spending a lot of time with April. The other horses are getting jealous."

Daniel snorted. "She'll keep them in their place." He tugged the reins loose from the fence rail and mounted. "Time us, will you?"

"As always, your wish is my command."

Eyeing his brother skeptically, Daniel settled his Stetson more firmly on his head. "Since when?"

"Since you started telling Ivy to get lost."

"Not lost, exactly. She's not my type. She's too young. Too clingy." Although a few years ago the waitress at the diner might have been. But not now. The kind of female that was looking for trouble no longer appealed to him.

The picture of Mindy walking into church with Aunt Martha popped into his head. A summery dress that skimmed her calves. Golden curls bouncing as she pushed her aunt along. Blue eyes that sparked like a summer wildfire, challenging him to keep his distance.

Like the upcoming riding events, he'd always loved a challenge.

Too bad she hadn't still been at the knitting shop when he went back to town for Arnie's prescription.

Daniel reined April into the ring where he'd set up an obstacle course—a low bridge to walk over, logs laid out in a path to be daintily stepped over, a rail to straddle. Although the trail event wasn't timed for speed, the time to finish the course was limited, and time penalties were added for every misstep or refusal the horse made.

"Okay, here we go." With the almost imperceptible pressure of his knees, he urged April toward the bridge.

"The clock is ticking," Arnie announced.

Without faltering, April went up and over the bridge. Daniel maneuvered her to the next obstacle, the row of logs, which she took with ease. Throughout the course, she didn't falter once. Even when he dangled the required bundle of burlap on a rope in front of her face, she didn't flinch.

They reached the end of the course, and Daniel

trotted April over to the fence. "How'd we do?" he asked Arnie.

"A perfect ride. More than two minutes under the limit, bro."

"Ha!" He gave April a congratulatory pat on her neck. "Eat your heart out, Charlie Moffett. This year you'll meet your match. And eat our dust."

Chapter Three

Monday morning, Melinda took her aunt to Manhattan for her three-times-weekly physical therapy appointment. When they got back home, it was time for lunch, followed by a much-needed nap for Aunt Martha.

Melinda gathered up a bucket, rolls of paper towels, plastic trash bags and cleaning supplies and carried them to the shop. The door opened much easier this time and she stepped inside.

A groan escaped her lips. Where to begin?

"Take your pick, Melinda Sue," she said aloud. The whole shop had to be cleaned up eventually.

Leaving the door open to let some fresh air in, she walked over to the cash register beside a glass case that displayed yarn winders and bobbins.

She'd checked the cash drawer on Saturday and found less than twenty dollars in change. Tugging a plastic box out from beneath the register that was crammed with file folders, she squatted down to go through the records.

Invoices from three years ago were mixed with even older records. None were noted as paid. A handwritten ledger showed checks written from 2001 through most of 2006 and a bank balance that wasn't worth writing home about. Hadn't Martha paid any bills since then? Maybe she'd switched to a different bank account.

Blowing out a discouraged sigh, she made a cursory examination of the rest of the business records, then set the box aside. She'd have to talk to Martha about the bookkeeping. Her time while Martha napped would be better spent cleaning and tossing what wasn't usable.

On her knees, she pulled everything out of the display case, set the items aside and used window cleaner on the neglected shelves and inside of the case. Years of grime darkened paper towels as one section of glass after another began to sparkle.

"Hello? Anybody here?"

Melinda started at the sound of Daniel's familiar voice.

"The shop's not open," she called from behind the counter.

"Your door is." His boots tramped across the wood floor until his long, jeans-clad legs materialized in front of the display case. "Hey, Goldilocks. Looks like you're hard at work."

"I am." She considered asking him if he'd enjoyed his date with April, but thought better of it. Instead, she squirted window cleaner on the next section of glass.

"Is Aunt Martha planning to reopen the shop?"

"We're thinking about it." She swirled the glass cleaner around, blurring her view of his legs.

"That a fact?" he drawled, an arrogant grin in his voice. "Want some help?"

She lifted her head too fast, whacking it on the inside of the display case. She rubbed the back of her skull.

"No! I'm fine." She looked up at him. Foolish woman! She should've known he'd be grinning at her, a wolfish grin, a grin that crinkled the corners of his eyes and made them flash with amusement.

"You got another one of those squirt bottles? I can do the outside of the case while you're working on the inside."

Trapped on the inside, he meant.

She wanted to tell him no, she didn't have another bottle of window cleaner. But he was just clever enough to look over the display case, spot her spare bottle and see that she was lying.

She reached for the bottle and tossed it up and over the case, following that with a roll of paper towels. "There you go, Swagger. Do your best."

"I intend to."

An odd shimmer of unease slid down her back. What did he mean by that? And did she want to know?

Over the next few minutes, she kept her head down and her hand moving on the glass. At one point, her hand and his were only the thickness of two paper towels and the glass apart. His heat seemed to burn right through the transparent barrier to her palm.

She snatched her hand back. Beads of sweat formed on her forehead.

"I wouldn't think Aunt Martha would be well enough

to keep the shop open by herself," Daniel commented in a casual tone.

"Probably not."

"She going to hire someone to help?"

Melinda sat back on her haunches and wiped her forehead with the back of her hand. "If you must know, I'm going to manage the shop for her."

"Yeah? You know enough about knitting to run this kind of operation?"

"I ran a very successful knitting shop in Pennsylvania until—" She clamped her mouth shut. She didn't want to finish the sentence. Daniel had no need to know about Jason. She didn't want his sympathy and didn't want to discuss the subject. The depth of her loss, her failure, was far too painful.

"Then I bet your aunt is happy you're staying in Potter Creek." He took a final swipe at the outside of the display case. "So am I."

She didn't respond. She couldn't. The sincerity in his lowered voice had nearly undone her. Her chin trembled. She tamped down the emotion welling in her chest as hard as she could and dug deep to find the protective shield that had kept her sane the past three years. A shield that kept the PTSD at bay most of the time.

She balled the damp paper towel in her fist. "Don't feel you have to stick around on my account. I'm sure April would be happy to see you," she said.

He laughed. A big, booming, masculine laugh that exploded from deep in his chest and bounced off the walls of the cluttered knitting shop.

Confusion knitted her brows. Why did he think her remark was so funny?

Standing, his grin unnerving her, he placed the glass cleaner and paper towel on the counter. "I'll be sure to give April your regards."

The rest of the week was a blur of taking Aunt Martha to physical therapy, scrubbing the shop clean and sorting yarn, creating bins of fifty-percent-off odd skeins and discarding others that had faded or become hopelessly tangled.

Invariably, sometime during the day Daniel showed up. Once he came with a bucket and a squeegee on a pole to clean the front window, inside and out.

Another day he came with a container of chili Arnie had made that he wanted taste-tested for the chili cook-off at the Potato Festival. Daniel stayed long enough to climb up a ladder to clean the ancient light fixtures and replace burned-out bulbs.

Aunt Martha and Melinda devoured the chili for dinner that night.

Melinda wasn't sure what Daniel was trying to accomplish. She hadn't given him any cause to think she was interested in him. On the contrary, she was often sharp with him. The fact that she'd begun to look forward to his arrival didn't mean a thing.

Or so she told herself.

She didn't want a relationship with anyone, certainly not with someone like Daniel, a consummate flirt and ladies' man.

A man who had always made her heart beat faster.

* * *

By the following Monday, Melinda declared she'd scrubbed, cleaned and sorted all she could. Now she needed new, fresh stock, which would enable her to hold a grand reopening next Saturday. Her dream was to someday add needlepoint to the inventory, but not yet. She had to get the yarn sales on a solid footing first.

She was on her cell phone, having placed an order for yarn and other supplies with a Denver wholesaler, when Daniel strolled into the shop. She acknowledged him with a quick lift of her hand, palm out, sending a message that she didn't want to be interrupted.

"I'm sure Aunt Martha's Knitting and Notions has had an account with you for many years," she said into the phone. "I've seen the invoices."

"I'm sorry, ma'am, but that account has been inactive for a long time," Jeff, the sales rep, replied.

"Well, then, let's reactivate the account, shall we? We're planning to reopen this Saturday and I need that merchandise. Please." She used her sweetest, most persuasive voice to cajole the man on the other end of the line.

"To reactivate the account, I'll need you to complete our credit forms and submit them. They're online at our website. You can download them."

Aware that Daniel was poking around the shop, flipping through pattern books, looking as relaxed as he would in a public library, Melinda gritted her teeth. "How long will it take to get them approved?"

"Two or three weeks is the usual time period."

She groaned and dropped her head into her hand. "Let me explain again, Jeff. I want to reopen the shop this Saturday. That's five days from now. I need the merchandise no later than Friday to stock the bins. I cannot wait two weeks for approval of credit."

"It often takes three weeks, ma'am."

Holding the phone away from her ear, and holding her temper in check, she looked up at the ceiling. She drew a steadying breath and brought the phone back to her ear.

"What do you suggest I do in the interim while you check our credit?"

"You could charge the merchandise to a personal credit card. We'd ship this afternoon and you'd have the delivery by Wednesday."

"A personal credit card." The words landed with a thud in her midsection. Since declaring bankruptcy, she'd been living on a cash basis. She didn't want to run up any personal debt. The one credit card she possessed had a very low limit, which she'd almost exceeded buying the airline ticket to Bozeman and hadn't paid that off yet. "I don't have my card handy," she hedged. "I'll have to check with the shop owner."

"I'd be happy to wait, ma'am."

That wasn't likely to help much. Aunt Martha seemed to be living on her Social Security, which was less than munificent. Assuming she had a credit card, Melinda doubted it had a high enough limit to cover the cost of the merchandise she'd ordered.

Daniel crossed the shop to the counter and handed her his credit card.

Gaping, she stared at the silver card embossed with Daniel's name and *O'Brien Ranch*. She shook her head.

"Ma'am, are you still there?"

"Uh, hang on a minute, Jeff." She covered the phone with her hand. "I can't use your card, Daniel," she whispered.

"Why not? You need the merchandise. When you get the shop open and doing business, you can pay me back."

"I'm buying more than a thousand dollars' worth of yarn and notions."

He lifted his shoulders in an easy shrug. "That's fine. Think of it as a loan."

"I may not be able to pay you back right away."

He touched her hair, twirling a finger through one of her curls. His lips curved ever so slightly with the hint of a smile. "We'll work it out."

Goose bumps sped down her spine and her knees went weak. She definitely shouldn't let him do this. It wasn't right for him to pay for what she couldn't afford. But if she didn't, how could she reopen the shop without a decent selection of yarn?

"Ma'am, did you want to call me back when you work something out?"

"No, I, uh…"

Daniel slipped the cell phone from her hand. "Hi, Jeff. I'm Daniel O'Brien, a friend of the shop owner. We'll put the charges on my card. How does that sound?" He winked at Melinda.

While she stood staring at him dumbstruck, Daniel reeled off all the necessary information to charge his card over a thousand dollars.

When he finished, he handed the phone back to her. "You're all set. Everything should arrive Wednesday and you'll be ready for Saturday's opening."

"You shouldn't have..." she stammered, her face flushing. "I mean, I shouldn't have let you—"

"The proper response is, 'Thank you, Daniel.'"

She closed her eyes to block out the intensity, the caring, she saw in his. Self-consciously, she fiddled with the same strand of hair that he'd twirled over his finger. "Thank you, Daniel."

"Good girl. Now what have we got to do to get ready for Saturday?"

She stepped back, trying to think, trying to blot out the gratitude that was making her act stupid and jumbled her thoughts as completely as a kitten could unwind a ball of yarn. She didn't deserve his kindness.

"I need to make up some flyers to post around town. A big sign for the shop's window." The gears in her brain that had stalled under Daniel's determined assault began clicking again. "Place an ad in the newspaper. Get a reporter to cover the opening."

"Sounds good. You get the flyers made and I'll deliver them to the stores in town, get the owners to post them in their windows."

"You don't have to do that."

"Sure I do. I need you to be a big success so I'll get my money back."

That sounded ever so logical except for one little problem: Melinda was pretty sure Daniel had a totally different agenda in mind.

Chapter Four

Freshly printed flyers and advertising copy in hand, Melinda headed on foot toward the office of the *Potter Creek Courier,* the town's semiweekly newspaper.

Aunt Martha's physical therapist had cut her back to one appointment per week, telling her she should keep up her daily exercises at home. Thoughtfully, a church friend of Martha's had volunteered to take her to the therapist this morning.

On a Monday, Main Street was quiet. Two preadolescent boys went racing by on their bikes, whooping and hollering, their baseball caps worn backward on their heads. By afternoon, they'd probably join other youngsters at the municipal pool at the far end of town.

Most of the vehicles on the road were pickups, often with a bale of hay in the back. Older women seemed to have a preference for cars rather than trucks, their gray heads barely high enough to see over the steering wheels, their speed a few miles per hour slower than the youthful bicyclists.

Older teens and young adults who had jobs or chores to do gathered later, near sundown, at the picnic area at Riverside Park. They'd swim in the wide spot in the river, listen to music played on boom boxes or from car stereos, make out behind the bushes.

Melinda's face warmed and her steps slowed at the memory of being with Daniel at the park. If she had known about DeeDee Pickens, she never would have gone to the park with him. Not even once.

She reached the building that housed the *Courier,* a one-story stucco structure with wooden siding that mimicked an old Western town. The headline on the most recent edition of the newspaper, which was posted in the front window, announced VFW Elects New Officers.

Hard to imagine any news more exciting than that in Potter Creek. Her lips twisted into a wry smile. Finding excitement hadn't been her goal by coming west.

Finding inner peace and starting over were closer to the truth.

The cowbell over the door clanked as she stepped inside and got a whiff of printer's ink and old newsprint. A stack of newspapers sat at one end of a long counter along with racks of Potter Creek postcards and area maps. The two desks behind the counter were both piled high with papers that threatened to topple over with the least provocation.

A woman appeared from the back room. Probably in her early fifties, she wore a bright, friendly smile.

"Morning. What can I do for you, hon?" she asked.

Melinda introduced herself and placed one of her

fuchsia flyers on the counter. "I'm Martha Raybin's great-niece. I'm going to be reopening Aunt Martha's Knitting and Notions, and I'd like to place an ad in the paper."

"Oh, I'd heard Martha's niece was in town helping her out. I'm Amy Thurgood, editor of the *Courier*." She moved her glasses from the top of her head, where they'd been perched, and slipped them on to study the flyer. The banner on the flyer read Grand Reopening on a background that resembled a knitted scarf with needles and yarn bordering the pertinent information. "Martha's a dear lady. Guess she had quite a fright with that stroke 'n' all."

"She seems to be recovering well."

"I'm so glad to hear that. Is this the ad you want to run?"

"Yes, I brought you a CD. I thought that'd be easiest for you rather than scanning the master copy." At the Pittsburgh knitting shop, one of Melinda's jobs as manager was to create and place their advertising in the local paper. She'd spent most of Sunday afternoon designing this ad and the flyer.

"Perfect."

"I was also hoping you might assign a reporter to cover our grand reopening."

"A reporter?" Amy looked over the top of her glasses at Melinda, her hazel eyes sparkling with good humor. "Hon, around here I'm the editor in chief, sole reporter and general gofer girl. I do have a couple of stringers who cover high school sports and write the Ag column for me. But what you see is what you get, all-round newspaper woman with printer's ink in her veins."

Chuckling, Melinda warmed to this outgoing woman. Potter Creek might not compare in size to Pittsburgh, but it certainly topped the big city for friendliness.

As they talked, she discovered a three-column ad would cost less than a third of the price the Pittsburgh paper charged, although it would still make a dent in her minuscule checking account. Amy promised to run the ad in both Wednesday's and Saturday's editions. She also volunteered to post a flyer in her front window and agreed to drop into the shop during the opening.

Amy pushed her glasses back to the top of her head. "So, are you planning to stay here and run the shop for Martha?"

"That's the plan." Fingers crossed that she could turn a profit and keep both her and her aunt from the poorhouse.

"I'm glad to hear that, hon. Folks in Potter Creek are turning pretty gray these days. We can use more young people who'll stick around and raise their families here."

An ache bloomed in Melinda's chest. "Aunt Martha is my only family." Her voice caught. She'd lost everyone she had loved, and the most precious of all, dead virtually by her own hand.

Once outside, Melinda drew a deep breath to clear her head and shake off her memories. Memories that ripped open her splintered heart. Memories that had the power to drive her to her knees if she let them.

Forcefully, she straightened her shoulders. She had to keep busy, had to keep her demons safely locked away.

As long as she was out and about, she'd drop off flyers at some of the local businesses, meet the owners and ask them to post the flyers. No need to wait for Daniel to do it.

No need at all.

Because the Potter Creek Diner was immediately next door to the newspaper office, Melinda decided to start there. Not only did they have a large plate-glass window perfect for displaying posters, but they might also have a community bulletin board inside.

From across the street she heard the happy laugh of a child. Without thinking, she turned to see a boy about five years old skipping along holding his mother's hand.

Pain as sharp as an arrow arched into her chest. Her breath lodged in her lungs. Her vision wavered.

No, not now! she silently pleaded. She had too much to do to have a panic attack. *Focus on the flyers. Aunt Martha's Knitting and Notions.* Anything except her child who would never laugh and skip again.

She whirled and fled into the diner. She forced herself to take a deep breath and expel the pain that had constricted her chest. She forced herself to focus on these new, *safe* surroundings, not on the past.

The interior decor of the diner had a Western flavor. At eye level, the paneled walls were covered with black-and-white photos of rodeo events and old-time cowboys. Above those were the stuffed heads of a moose with giant antlers, a cougar with hungry yellow eyes, a snarling wolf and a sad-eyed buffalo.

Dragging her gaze away from the four sets of accusing eyes, she noticed that only two tables were occupied at this midmorning hour, both by middle-aged couples having a late breakfast. An original watercolor painting mounted in a rustic frame hung on the wall behind them. The painting depicted magnificent, snow-covered Rocky Mountains, yet the eye was drawn to the tiny abstract figure of a woman standing alone in a meadow. Despite the beauty all around her, the solitary woman appeared isolated and forlorn.

The aura of sadness in the painting touched Melinda's heart as she realized that she could have been that unnamed figure.

Turning from the painting, Melinda approached a woman who sat at the end of the counter, sipping coffee from a mug and reading a paperback book. "Excuse me, I'm looking for the owner or manager of the diner."

The woman lifted her head and swivelled around. Melinda's eyes widened briefly as she recognized the flirtatious brunette she'd seen making a play for Daniel on the church basketball court.

"Pop isn't here right now. What can I do for you?"

"I, um, I wanted to put up, um, one of these flyers in your window." Melinda's tongue had apparently developed a bad case of nerves, making her sound like a stammering fool.

The woman turned her book facedown to save her place and held out her hand. "Lemme see."

Melinda passed her a flyer, noting the young woman

had wide, nearly black eyes and wore a touch of eye shadow that enhanced their size. No older than twenty, the girl was way too young for Daniel.

"Knitting, huh? I never learned how to knit. Didn't see much point."

"I'm going to offer both beginning and advanced classes. The basics are really easy. You'd be surprised how quickly you could learn to make scarves and caps, even sweaters like this one." She'd intentionally worn a light-weight, vest-style sweater in bright colors as a sample of what she'd be teaching to advanced students.

The woman glanced at the flyer again and shrugged. "Sure, you can put it up in the window. Don't know that you'll get many takers."

"Hey, Ivy," a man called from one of the tables. "You got any more coffee over there?"

"Sure, sure. Hang on a sec." Ivy handed back the flyer. "Go ahead. Put it up if you want."

Her lack of enthusiasm did nothing to bolster Melinda's confidence. She opened her mouth to thank Ivy, but the young woman was already off her stool heading for the coffeepot simmering on the burner behind the counter.

She tried to repress a surge of annoyance. Or was it jealousy? In either case, it didn't matter. She'd accomplished what she'd wanted. She could put up the flyer.

Placing the flyer on the window right next to the door, she held it with one hand while she pulled off a few inches of tape and smoothed it across the top of the sheet. She did the same along the bottom, then looked up only to be snared by a familiar pair of dark eyes.

Daniel. Standing on the other side of the window.

Gasping, she took a step back, nearly knocking over a chair that was behind her.

The man had an annoying habit of popping up out of nowhere when she least expected to see him.

His eyes crinkled with a smile and he winked at her.

Her stomach took a tumble. Confound his hide.

Before she knew it, he'd stepped inside the diner and was standing right next to her.

"Hey, there, Goldilocks. I thought that was my job, putting up the flyers."

"I was just next door—"

"Hey, Danny!" Ivy cried. "Didn't expect to see you this morning." She hurried across the diner, all smiles and puppy-eager. "You want some bacon and eggs or a stack of pancakes this morning?"

"Uh, no, thanks. I already ate." He glanced back to Melinda. "I'll buy you a cup of coffee if you want."

She lifted her chin. "No, I'd better get on with putting up these flyers. Got to get the word out, you know."

"I just made a fresh pot of coffee," Ivy announced, her smile now frozen on her face. Straight white teeth surrounded by rictus lips painted a pale pink.

"Maybe later," Daniel said to Ivy, then took the flyers from Melinda's hand. "I'll come with you, introduce you around."

"That isn't necessary." She reached for the door-knob.

Daniel's big hand got there first. He opened the door.

She had little choice but to precede him out onto the sidewalk.

"Catch you later, Ivy," he said as he joined Melinda outside. "Where to first?"

She remained frozen in place, a slow burn building in her stomach. "You still have women falling all over themselves for you, don't you? Just like ten years ago."

He lifted his shoulders in a careless shrug. "I haven't noticed you falling all over me."

Not recently, at any rate. "Ivy started hyperventilating the moment you walked in the diner. And then there's April. Does she know Ivy's after you?"

A low chuckle rumbled in his chest and he hooked his arm across Melinda's shoulders, urging her down the sidewalk. "April doesn't have a jealous bone in her body, if that's what you're asking."

She bristled. "I wasn't asking."

"Good, because April's my one true love and smartest mare in my breeding stock."

Melinda dug in her heels. "Your breeding stock?" What on earth—

"I raise quarter horses, Mindy, and breed them." His lips kicked up into another grin. "One day you'll have to come out to the ranch. I'll introduce you to April. You'll love her."

Her jaw went slack. As though he'd poured cold water on a raging wildfire, the burning sensation in her stomach vanished, leaving a residual of confusion. She frowned.

"You wouldn't lie to me, would you?"

"Not about April."

Which meant he might lie about something else?

He guided her into a real-estate office and introduced her to Rick Jennings, a tall, lanky man in his forties. "This is Aunt Martha's niece. She's reopening the knitting shop."

Cordial and friendly, Nate welcomed her to town and was happy to put the flyer in his window.

Next came the grocery store. Melinda had picked up fresh produce there a couple of times in the past week, although she'd done her major shopping at the supermarket in Manhattan while Aunt Martha had her physical therapy session.

Daniel reintroduced her to Art Williams, the grocery store owner, whom she recalled from the summer she'd spent in town. She'd bought a lot of ice cream bars and bottles of soda in his store. He'd aged some in the past ten years and lost a good deal of hair, but he still had the look of Ichabod Crane with his narrow face and prominent Adam's apple.

"Oh, I remember this sweet little lady," he said with a knowing look. "Remember you taking a liking to her right off, too, Danny boy."

Heat flooded her cheeks. Had her relationship with Daniel been that obvious? Evidently.

Daniel simply grinned and thumbed his Stetson farther back on his head. "You've always had a good memory, Art."

Quickly deciding to take control of the conversation, Melinda explained about the flyer. When Art gave his permission to post the flyer in his window, she yanked one from Daniel's hand and marched to the front of the store.

She felt Daniel staring at her, and her ears burned fiery hot as she taped the flyer to the window.

Enough was enough. She didn't need an escort for this job. If Daniel wanted to spread the flyers around town, it was fine with her.

"I have to get home to check on my aunt." She handed Daniel the roll of tape. "You can drop off any extra flyers at the shop. Just slide them through the mail slot and I'll pick them up later."

His finely arched brows rose. "You running out on me again?"

Guilt for the cowardly way she'd left ten years ago without confronting Daniel about DeeDee pricked her conscience. "I'm checking on Aunt Martha." She tossed her hair behind her shoulder. "If you don't have time to distribute the flyers, I'll take care of them later."

He leaned a shoulder against the side of the open door. "You've turned into a prickly little thing, haven't you?"

Only when it comes to you, Daniel O'Brien.

She held out her hand for the flyers.

He pushed himself upright. "I'll have the town painted with flyers in no time. You go on and look after Aunt Martha."

"Fine." She plopped the tape into his hand, whirled and struck out at a quick pace for the relative safety of Martha's house.

Not that she'd be safe anywhere with Mr. Bad Boy

O'Brien on the prowl. He made her feel things she didn't want to feel, things she had no right to feel.

Daniel watched Mindy walk away. *Prickly* didn't begin to describe her attitude these days. Oh, she was attracted to him. Her quick blushes and the way she kept him at arm's length told him that.

But there was something else going on, too. She didn't smile as much as she used to. And he had yet to hear her laugh, the lyrical sound that had reminded him of water flowing over a rocky creek bed on a lazy summer afternoon.

Maybe she was still grieving for her late husband. He could understand that. She was the kind of woman who didn't give her heart easily. Whoever the guy was, he must've been something special for her to have married him.

Lucky, too.

Ten years ago, Daniel hadn't been man enough to hang on to her. He'd been trying to prove he was wilder, more no-account than his old man. Ten years ago, she'd been smart enough not to stick around with him.

He didn't know about now. One thing he'd learned by raising and training quarter horses was patience.

He'd have to give it some time and see how it all played out.

It took Daniel about an hour to deliver the flyers to the businesses on Main Street. When he discovered Mindy wasn't at the knit shop, he was tempted to return the flyers to her at her aunt's house, then thought better of it.

Too much pressure on a show horse made him, or her, balk. Mindy was already high-strung. He'd give her a rest.

For now.

He slipped the remaining flyers into the mail slot and let them fall to the floor. April was waiting for him back at the ranch. So were a whole lot of chores.

He'd come up with a new tactic to breach the barriers Goldilocks had raised and save that for another day.

Chapter Five

Melinda barely slept Friday night. Instead, she tossed and turned, her head filled with worries about the grand reopening Saturday.

Did she have enough chunky-weight yarn in stock? Montana winters were frigid.

Older women, of which there were plenty in Potter Creek, loved to knit for their grandchildren. Maybe she should have ordered more baby-weight yarn in more colors.

If a lot of people signed up for beginning classes, did she have enough needles on hand to get them started?

Had she ordered enough tea sandwiches from the bakery? Had she bought enough fruit punch and paper cups?

She flopped over onto her stomach.

Why hadn't she seen Daniel since Monday? Had he given up on her?

Which was exactly what she wanted, right?

With the first hint of sunrise, Melinda gave up trying

to sleep and staggered out of bed. Either the reopening would be a success or it wouldn't. She'd done all she could and now it was up to the Lord to help her out.

If He was willing. *If* He had forgiven her.

She dressed and had breakfast ready for Aunt Martha when she got up.

"Today's the day, dear." Using her walker, Aunt Martha made slow but steady progress into the kitchen. "Aren't you excited?"

"Terrified, actually." Melinda held out a chair at the kitchen table for Martha and brought her a cup of coffee.

"Oh, my, I don't think you have a thing to worry about, dear. Several of my friends have promised they'll drop by to visit with us. They're anxious to see what changes you've made in the shop."

But would her friends buy any yarn? Melinda wondered. It might have been better if she'd reopened the shop in the fall. People thought about knitting projects during cool weather, not during the blazing days of summer.

Not that she could fast-forward the calendar anyway. In any event, she needed a job and some income now.

She served up a bowl of oatmeal with raisins and placed it in front of Martha along with a slice of buttered toast.

"Aren't you having any breakfast, dear?"

"No, coffee's fine for me. I'm afraid if I eat anything, I'll throw up."

"Nonsense." She patted the chair beside her. "You can't start such an important day without a good breakfast. Your mother would say the same thing if she were here."

"I suppose she would." But her mother wasn't there. She and her father had died in a car crash eight years ago. The autopsy revealed her father had had a heart attack and lost control of the car. Melinda had always felt her mother would have wanted to die at her husband's side. Their love for each other had been that strong.

When she married Joe, she had prayed they would develop that powerful a bond. Her prayers hadn't been answered. While she had loved him, it wasn't the all-consuming love that he deserved. He'd sensed that and so had his family. She'd failed him just as she'd failed their son.

She managed to gag down a slice of toast, help Aunt Martha to dress and cleaned up the kitchen. For the grand reopening, Melinda draped a bell-pattern shawl around her shoulders as a sample of her knitting.

It was still well before ten o'clock, the time set to open the shop, but she wanted to be there early enough for a last-minute check of her supplies.

Because the path between Martha's house and the shop wasn't paved and difficult for the wheelchair to maneuver, she helped her aunt into the car, loaded the wheelchair and walker in the trunk and drove around the block. She parked in front of the shop. The Grand Reopening banner hung listlessly in the still morning air.

Inside, everything seemed to be in order. Skeins of yarn were neatly organized in their bins. New pattern books were on display. Notions were sorted and an ample selection available.

On a new corkboard, which Daniel had hung for her, she'd displayed a few ideas for altruistic knitting projects—knitted caps for hospital newborns, afghans for Afghanistan, lap robes for Wounded Warriors, U.S. soldiers who had returned from battlefields around the world. Beside that she posted a sign-up sheet for both morning and late-afternoon knitting classes.

Now all Melinda needed was a few dozen eager customers with money in their wallets and she'd be all set.

By eleven o'clock, Melinda was near panic. Except for the delivery boy from the bakery with the tea sandwiches, not another soul had crossed the threshold to enter Aunt Martha's Knitting and Notions.

Martha didn't seem at all concerned. She just chatted on about her friends. "Rose Hemingway said she'd drop by. She lives just south of town. Lovely family. Four or five children, I can never keep track. Must have a dozen grandchildren by now. She's always showing pictures of them."

"Does she do a lot of knitting?"

"Not anymore. Arthritis, don't you know. Her poor fingers are all gnarled with it. She has some sort of a cream she puts on her hands, but I don't know how much it helps the pain, poor dear."

Melinda's hopes plummeted as she learned that Agnes Moore was losing her sight to macular degeneration, Sylvia Goodsend seemed to be slipping into senility and Martha's longtime friend Bea Farnsworth had developed a heart problem.

None of them seemed like potential customers for yarn and notions.

Finally, when it was almost noon, women began to show up in twos and threes. Melinda was so relieved that she nearly gushed trying to explain her vision for the shop. A place for friends to gather and chat while they worked on their own projects. A *community* of knitters and eventually those who enjoyed doing needlepoint.

Amy Thurgood from the *Courier* dropped by while she was talking to two women but she didn't stay long. She just waved, mouthed "Good luck" and left again.

By three o'clock the tea sandwiches had vanished and she had only a half gallon of punch left. She sent Aunt Martha home in the care of one of her friends from her Bible study group and told her to rest. She'd looked exhausted from all the activity and conversation.

As for the grand reopening, Melinda had sold a rousing $22.36 worth of merchandise for her efforts, which didn't even cover the cost of the punch.

Hot, tired and discouraged, she sat down at the big table in the back of the shop and put her head in her hands.

"Hey, Goldilocks, where's all the excitement?"

Melinda went rigid, a mix of relief, pleasure and annoyance at her reaction to Daniel's arrival momentarily paralyzing her.

"If you're looking for excitement," she mumbled, head still in her hands, "you've come to the wrong place."

He pulled out a chair next to her, swung it around and straddled it. "The opening didn't go so well?" His lowered voice vibrated with warmth and sympathy.

She peered at him out of the corner of her eye. No man had a right to look so virile, the angles and planes of his face so sharply defined, his shoulders so broad. His well-worn Stetson tipped back on his head completed the macho image. It simply wasn't fair to a woman on the verge of tears who wanted to throw herself into his arms.

"Hard to consider twenty-two dollars for a day's work a great success." Tears clogged her throat, her voice so strained it sounded as if it was snared on a buttonhook.

He placed his hand on her shoulder and gently rubbed her back. The heat of his palm seeped through the cotton fabric of her blouse, making her feel even more vulnerable than she had a minute ago.

"How 'bout the classes? Anyone sign up?"

"Not a soul."

"Maybe they'll show up when the time comes."

"Maybe." Believing that would take more faith than she could muster.

"I know what would perk you right up." He stood and flipped the chair back around. "I'll buy you an ice cream cone at the diner."

She lifted her head and gaped at him. No way was she going to traipse into Ivy's domain for a cone or anything else. Not with Daniel, at any rate.

"No, thanks. I'd rather have you round up a dozen

or so knitters with money to spend on yarn. Besides, I can't leave the shop until five o'clock closing time."

He blew out a breath and tucked his fingertips in his hip pockets. "Because you're expecting a late rush of customers?"

"Because the sign on the door says the shop stays open until five."

He grunted noncommittally and paced over to the cork board where the blank sign-up sheet hung like a white flag of surrender.

He did an about-face. "Okay, if you won't come with me, I'll bring the ice cream to you."

"You don't have to—"

"Chocolate or pistachio?"

She sighed. She'd had only a piece of toast and one tea sandwich all day. Her growling stomach provided the answer. "Definitely chocolate."

His grin resembled that of *Alice in Wonderland*'s Cheshire cat. "Don't go away. I'll be back before you know it."

With that he went out the door and jogged up the street, leaving Melinda shaking her head. The man was a force of nature, one she'd barely been able to resist ten years ago.

Apparently her ability to withstand his potent appeal hadn't improved over the years.

At least he'd been able to get a smile out of Mindy, Daniel thought later as he drove back to the ranch. Or more likely, it was the double-dark chocolate that had brought a smile to her lips.

He parked the truck by the barn and went inside through the back door. Arnie was in the kitchen, the rich aroma of chili cooking on the stove mouth-watering. A year or so after the accident, they'd ripped out the whole kitchen and put in new granite counters and a stove that were more easily accessible for Arnie in his wheelchair. He'd pretty well taken over all the cooking, which was fine by Daniel.

"Here, taste this." Arnie held out a spoonful of chili.

Daniel took the spoon from him. "Haven't you fussed with your recipe enough? I thought the last batch was terrific and, frankly, I'm getting a little tired of a straight diet of chili night after night."

"Chili's good for you. Rich in protein and fiber. Besides, I put a little something extra in this batch. I want to see what you think."

With a shrug, Daniel put the spoonful of chili in his mouth and started to chew. Two seconds later, the burn of chili peppers brought tears to his eyes. His tongue registered a sweet taste at the same time his lips started to sting.

He grabbed for a glass, filled it with water from the tap and gulped it down. Breathing hard, he shook his head. "What're you trying to do, bro? Poison the entire town? Or just melt the lining of their stomachs?"

Arnie's dark brows flattened. "Too much, huh?"

"Yeah, you could say that." He grabbed another glass of water, drinking it more slowly. "You could get arrested for arson with that stuff."

A smile hovered around the corners of his lips.

"Perfect. Then that's the recipe I'll enter in the Red Hot Division at the Potato Festival."

"You'd be better off to pour it down a prairie-dog hole. It'd wipe out the entire prairie-dog population in six counties."

"Ha. Just because your itty-bitty taste buds are so sensitive, doesn't mean everyone wants to eat pap. You watch, this year I'll be a double winner in the chili cook-off."

"Yeah, well, if that's what we're having for dinner, I'll fix myself a peanut butter sandwich. I value my taste buds too much to burn them off with a blowtorch." He tossed his hat on the kitchen table, sat down and pulled out his cell phone. He punched in the number of Becca McCall. He was in charge of the church youth group and she was the current president.

"Hey, Becca," he said when she answered. "It's Daniel. You got a minute?"

"Sure. What's up?" A redheaded sixteen-year-old with an energetic personality, her voice pinged the decibel limit on Daniel's cell. He held the phone away from his ear.

"You know how you kids have been trying to come up with some kind of a project for the summer? I think I've got one for us."

"Great. What is it?"

"The gal who's managing Aunt Martha's knitting shop has some good ideas about making afghans for Afghanistan or knitting sweaters and caps for the kids. It looks like an easy thing everyone could do."

Silent for a moment, Becca finally said, "I don't

know how to knit, and I don't think the guys will go for the idea."

"Hey, that's the beauty of it. Melinda, the manager, is going to teach us how to knit. If the kids don't want to make stuff for the kids in Afghanistan, we can make lap robes for our own wounded troops that come home and are hospitalized."

"Well, I'm not…"

"Talk it up with the kids, would you? I'm going to learn to knit and so is my brother. It'll be fun."

Arnie wheeled his chair around. "No way, Danny. I'm not going to take up knitting."

Daniel waved off his comment. "Not only would we be doing some good for others, we'd be helping a local business get on its feet."

"Okay," she said. "If you and Arnie are going to do it, I guess the guys will go along with the idea."

"Great." He gave her the details about the Tuesday and Thursday classes scheduled for late afternoons. "You can let me know what they think tomorrow at church."

As soon as he disconnected, Arnie resumed his complaint.

"I'm not going learn to knit. You're crazy. Why would I want to do something like that?"

"You're going to do it 'cause Melinda Spencer and her knit shop are going to fold if she can't attract some serious business. I loaned her more than a thousand bucks and I need for her to pay me back."

Arnie's mouth dropped open. "You what?"

Daniel picked up his hat and ran his fingertips around

the brim, not looking at his brother. "I charged some of her merchandise on our credit card. The wholesaler wouldn't give her credit."

"Oh, man… We can't afford… We got the mortgage coming due." Arnie groaned.

"Don't worry about it. She'll pay me back."

"You've really got it bad, don't you?"

Standing, Daniel put his hat on. "Just doing my Christian duty by helping out a friend. Worst case, I can use my winnings from the Potato Festival to make the mortgage payment."

"You'd better win both events, then," Arnie warned. "If we can't cover the balloon payment that's due in a month, we'll have to sell off half the herd. Otherwise the bank will take over everything except the shirts on our backs."

"You worry too much, bro. No way is Charlie Moffett going to beat me and April this year. Which means come foaling season the O'Brien ranch will be on top of the food chain."

"If we still own the ranch then."

From his incredulous expression and tone of voice, Arnie was skeptical. But Daniel hadn't had much choice about loaning Mindy the money.

He wanted to give her every reason to stay right here in Potter Creek for as long as possible. Then he'd see where they stood, see if she'd give him a second chance.

Something about her had called to him ten years ago. That same siren song had grown louder and more demanding since she'd come back to town.

She was like an alpha female in a wolf pack, strong and confident, a leader in her own right. His instinctual urge to be her alpha male, to travel beside her, protecting her, came from a place he'd never before visited. His heart.

Chapter Six

The stress of not searching for Daniel at church on Sunday made Melinda's neck ache from holding her head so rigid. Even so, her gaze kept honing in on him like a mosquito seeks out every square inch of bare skin.

When she and Aunt Martha arrived, Melinda had spotted Daniel in the parking lot talking to a teenage girl. A cute little redhead, she was way too young for him despite the adoration in her eyes.

Later she saw him on the opposite side of the church passing the collection plate. What had caused such a profound change in Daniel over the past ten years? During that time, she'd been driven to her knees with grief. In contrast, he appeared to have risen above who he had been. Had finding God made the difference in him while she had lost her way with the Lord?

At one point, she thought she identified his rich baritone voice singing a hymn, blending with her soprano in their own private duet.

She finally concluded that some mad scientist had cloned Daniel and there were dozens of him, which explained why his presence was so ubiquitous in Potter Creek. And why she seemed to have gone mad herself.

By the time the service was over, she realized she hadn't heard a word the preacher had spoken.

Another black mark for her on the Lord's checklist.

And never once all morning had Daniel sought her out.

Back home, Melinda fixed lunch for herself and Aunt Martha.

"You need some time off, Mindy," Martha said. She'd worn a navy print dress to church that highlighted her blue eyes. "Why don't you call one of the girls you got to know when you were here last time?"

"I hardly remember any of their names. Don't worry about me." She'd been far more focused on Daniel ten years ago than any of the girls she'd met. She certainly had no interest in calling him.

"Well, you can't spend every minute looking after me and the shop. Let me think." Martha ate a bite of the tomato-and-lettuce sandwich on wheat toast that Melinda had prepared. "There's Debbie Phillips. She married a boy over in Manhattan. Don Neff. I think they have a couple of youngsters. I'm sure she'd be happy if you dropped by to visit."

Melinda shook her head. "She's probably forgotten all about me. If I knew her, I can't remember her now." Worse, visiting a happy couple and their children would simply bring back too many painful memories and throw her into the grandmother of all panic attacks.

Eating her serving of cottage cheese on a sliced fresh peach, Martha was silent for a few moments.

"I know," she said. "There was a sweet girl. Ellie James, I think was her name. She came around a couple of times while you were here and I taught her to knit at the shop."

Smiling, Melinda remembered Ellie. She was a wild one, up for any adventure the guys had in mind, from climbing the cliffs at the river and diving off to a midnight swim or calf-roping contest. She hadn't lasted long in the knitting class. That had been her mother's idea. Knitting was too sedentary for Ellie's style. She'd preferred an activity that gave her an adrenaline rush. Even on her wildest day, Melinda hadn't been able to keep up with her. Still, they had enjoyed each other's company.

"Does Ellie still live around here?" Melinda asked.

"Well, now, let me think. Her mother's still living in the old ranch house, but her father passed away not too long ago. Now that I think of it…" Martha shook her head. "I think Ellie moved to Washington sometime back. She may visit once in a while, but I haven't seen her in an age."

Melinda's shoulders slumped with disappointment. "That's too bad. I would've enjoyed seeing her again." Probably by now Ellie had settled down and had a houseful of kids. That had been Melinda's dream, as well. But she'd been given little time to make that dream into a reality.

"I do worry about you, dear. You uprooted yourself from your friends to come here to help me out. Maybe you should call—"

"Aunt Martha, by the time Jason died I'd lost touch with most of my friends. They were uncomfortable around me, knowing what Jason was going through. It was almost as though they thought he was contagious and their own children could catch whatever he had." Her chin trembled. She remembered feeling so terribly alone.

Martha took Melinda's hand. "Are you sure they deserted you? Or did you isolate yourself because you couldn't bear to be around people who didn't have to carry the same burdens you did?"

Covering her mouth with her fingertips, Melinda shook her head. Had she really been that self-centered? "I don't know."

"Sometimes, dear, you have to ask others for help before help can be given."

Monday morning, Daniel parked his truck at the curb in front of the knit shop. Melinda watched as he began pulling long boards of lumber from the truck bed and dropping them on the sidewalk.

She went to the door and stood watching him, her arms crossed over her chest. "What are you doing?"

A two-by-four board dropped to the ground with a bang. "I'm building you a ramp so your shop's wheelchair accessible."

"Oh." She let one arm relax but continued to hold her

opposite arm with her hand. Now that she thought about it, getting Aunt Martha over the raised threshold in her wheelchair had been difficult. "That's very thoughtful of you. Thank you."

"You're welcome. Figured Aunt Martha would need this." Grinning, he unhooked a metal measuring tape from his belt. "I aim to please."

He squatted to measure the width of the doorsill.

Before taking a step back, she looked up and down the sidewalk as though expecting to see hordes of customers en route to the shop. "How long is this going to take?"

"Not long. An hour or so."

She supposed he wouldn't interfere with her customers, assuming any stopped by in the next hour.

Before long, Daniel was hard at work with a portable power saw, hammer and nails constructing the ramp. She noted he worked with care, no false cuts, no hammered thumbs to slow him down.

He'd be a handy man to have around the house.

Throwing up a mental Stop sign, she put that thought aside in a hurry and tried to look busy checking her inventory. She didn't want him to think she was gawking at him every minute.

It seemed as though it took him no time at all to complete his task.

"You're all set," he announced from the doorway. "I'll come by in a day or two with some wood sealer so the ramp will last in any weather."

"Thank you. I—" She hopped off the stool behind the counter where she'd been sitting. "Would you like a cup of coffee? I could—"

"No time today. Arnie's after me to help him move the herd to the upper pasture that hasn't been grazed this season. Maybe another time."

"Sure."

He tossed the leftover lengths of lumber into the truck, gave her a wave and drove off up the street.

Muttering to herself, she got out a broom to sweep up the sawdust he'd left behind. "How am I supposed to know what that man is after? First he ignores me, then he does something really thoughtful. Talk about mixed signals."

The rest of Monday crept by with only two customers visiting the shop, but they each bought two skeins of baby yarn. Melinda tried to take that as a good sign as she listened with one ear to the country-and-western songs playing softly on the radio on the shelf behind the cash register.

By Tuesday afternoon, she'd finished the sweater she'd started a year ago and had brought with her from Pittsburgh. She began to wonder what she ought to make next. Maybe a warm winter sweater for Daniel. She certainly had plenty of yarn to choose from.

Better yet, she could start on projects she could sell. If the good ladies of Potter Creek didn't want to knit, maybe they'd buy well-crafted garments.

She glanced at the clock on the wall. Almost four o'clock. In the faint hope someone would show up for the beginning knitting class, she'd put out some sample patterns, needles and yarn on the table at the back of the store.

Hearing some voices outside the door, a tiny bit of hope expanded in her chest and she put on an expectant face.

To her amazement, the redheaded teenager she'd seen talking with Daniel at church stepped inside followed by a girlfriend.

"Hello, girls. May I help you?"

They both looked around and shrugged. "Daniel said he'd be here," the redhead said.

"Daniel?" Melinda questioned. As in Daniel O'Brien?

"Yeah," she confirmed. "For the knitting class."

Melinda's brows rose and she blinked twice. Pleasure lifted her spirits like the sun after a storm passes. Daniel had sent these girls to learn how to knit? That was very sweet of him and unexpected. Had he always been that thoughtful and she hadn't noticed? He'd seemed so self-absorbed ten years ago. Melinda had been, too, if she was honest with herself.

Just then two teenaged boys lurched into the shop. "Hey, Becca. Marti. This is the place, huh?"

"I guess," Becca said.

"Well, now, this is wonderful," Melinda stammered. "Come in, please. All of you. You can look around first or sit over—"

The sound of a van door slamming out front preceded the sight of a man in a wheelchair rolling up the ramp with a dog trotting along behind him. The man wheeled into the shop with such ease, she could only wonder at the strength of his arms.

Melinda gaped at him, the dog and then at Daniel, who entered right behind the golden retriever and his brother, Arnie.

"Hi, gang," Daniel said. "Glad to see you guys made it. Are there more coming?"

"Frank's coming because Patti promised to be here," Becca said.

Daniel gave the girl a thumbs-up.

Maneuvering his way through the crowded shop, Arnie found a space at the table in the back. His beautiful dog immediately sat down, watching her master alertly. A trained service dog, Melinda realized.

Just then two more girls came into the shop, giggling. A boy showed up a moment later.

The kids laughed and joked with each other, their conversation filling the shop with their good spirits, accented occasionally with a friendly elbow jab, one boy to another. Virtually all were dressed in jeans and T-shirts, the girls' tops a bit more stylish than the boys.

Melinda edged her way over to Daniel. "Did you have to bribe these kids to come to knitting class?"

His lips quirked into his trademark grin. "Only Arnie. I had to promise I'd muck out all the horse stalls for a week."

Arnie wheeled around. "Hey, bro. Our deal was for a week of mucking for every class you drag me to."

Unable to repress her own smile, she extended her

hand to Arnie. "In that case, I hope you'll come to two classes a week. Maybe that would keep Daniel out of trouble for a while."

"Unlikely." Arnie took her hand, his palm rough with calluses. "Welcome back to Potter Creek, Mindy. I think my brother missed you."

"Yes, well…" A flush warmed her cheeks. "You've got a beautiful dog."

Arnie rested his hand on the dog's back. "This is Sheila, my best girl. I couldn't get along without her."

In response, Sheila's tail swept across the floor.

"I understand April is Daniel's best girl," Melinda said.

"The O'Brien brothers are great at attracting women who'll wag their tails or jump over obstacle courses for us," Arnie said with a self-deprecating laugh.

Melinda sensed that Arnie's paralysis slowed him down very little when it came to women. However, she was saddened by the accident that had left him wheelchair-bound.

Daniel said, "The kids are from the church youth group. They need a service project for the summer. I saw the ideas you'd posted on the bulletin board. They voted to give it a try. They've got a small treasury to cover expenses, so the group will buy the yarn and whatever else they need."

"That's…wonderful." Mentally, she added up the yarn and notions they'd need and smiled with relief. Some of the youngsters might even develop a long-term interest in knitting. "Thank you."

"No problem." Taking off his hat, he perched it on top of the display rack filled with patterns. His thick, dark hair retained the imprint of his hat circling his head. "Arnie and I will pay for our own."

"You mean *you'll* pay for both of us," Arnie countered.

"I'll give you a discount," she quickly said.

"I'll take that deal," Daniel said.

She turned toward the students. "All right, everyone, why don't you all gather around the table. It doesn't look like I have enough chairs, but there are a couple of folding chairs in the back room and a stool behind the counter."

"Frank, go find the chairs," Daniel ordered. "If there aren't enough chairs to go around, the guys can sit on the floor."

The boys groaned and one went jogging toward the storeroom.

Eventually, the group settled down and looked up at Melinda expectantly.

"I understand you want to learn to knit as part of doing a service project."

"I already know how to knit," a girl with a pixie face said. "I want to make a baby's cap for my sister. She's expecting in November."

"The rest of us thought knitting lap robes for wounded soldiers would a good project," Becca said.

There was a murmur of agreement around the room.

"That's an excellent project," Melinda agreed. "When

the lap robe is complete and ready to send, you can put a note or card inside for the soldier so he knows you care about him. He might even write back to you."

"That'd be awesome," a boy commented.

The girl who wanted to make a baby cap for her expected niece or nephew looked displeased with the lap robe decision, fidgeting with a strand of her blond hair.

"What's your name?" Melinda asked.

"Grace. Grace Staples."

Melinda eased her way past a couple of kids to get closer to Grace. "Tell you what, this is a much larger class than I can teach by myself. Since you know how to knit, you can be my assistant and help your friends learn the basics they'll need to make the lap robe squares. And if you can come in a bit early next time, I'll work with you and show you how to make a cap for the baby."

Her eyes brightened and she perked right up. "Would you?"

"Of course. I'd really appreciate your help, too."

She smiled and shrugged, looking around the table. "That means the guys will have to listen to me and not be all smart-alecky, doesn't it?"

Melinda glanced at Daniel, who nodded his approval.

"Absolutely, Grace. No smart alecks allowed," Melinda said.

The boys groaned again. The girls giggled.

Feeling very much in her element, Melinda rounded up some suitable yarn. "We want to make the lap robe out of yarn that is machine-washable and can go in the dryer. Take a look at the label on these skeins. The first thing you need to know is how to read the labels so you won't buy the wrong kind of yarn for whatever project you're doing."

The kids grabbed for the skeins, and she explained the symbols on the label. Then she let them choose the colors they wanted to use. They picked a three-color scheme of lime-green, forest-green and royal-blue that complemented each other and wouldn't easily show soil.

Next came winding the balls of yarn.

Trying desperately not to laugh at some of their unco-ordinated efforts, Melinda helped the pairs of young-sters who managed to tangle their yarn into impossible knots.

"Hey, don't make it so hard, kids." Daniel was work-ing with one of the girls and they seemed to be getting the job done without much trouble. "Think of it as wind-ing your fishing line on the reel."

Some of the boys didn't look convinced.

With Sheila sitting beside him, Arnie seemed to be doing fine with his partner. "I think they had me doing this kind of stuff in rehab. Not exactly rocket science, guys."

Melinda distributed knitting needles and had just started showing them the double cast-on method when she glanced at the wall clock. It was already after six. The time had raced by.

"I'm afraid casting on will have to wait until next time, kids. Can you all come back Thursday?"

Everyone nodded. Melinda gathered up the balls of yarn and needles and put them in a box for safe-keeping.

As the youngsters made their way out the door, she made it a point to thank each one for coming and encouraged them about their progress.

Arnie rolled up to the door, Sheila close behind him. "Good job, Mindy. Even the guys were really getting into this knitting business."

"They probably didn't want the girls to outdo them."

"Whatever works," he said with a laugh. He waved and rolled down the ramp to the van parked at the curb.

Daniel strolled up beside her. "You're good with kids."

"I like young people. They all seemed very nice."

"They are." He put his hat on and ran his hand along the brim, shaping it. "Write up an invoice for next time and I'll see to it that you get a check."

"I feel a little guilty taking their money."

"Don't. It's part of their service commitment." He stepped to the door. "I'll see you Thursday."

"I'll be here."

He turned to leave, then thought better of it. "The Potato Festival starts a week from Saturday. If you come, I'll introduce you to April. You can watch us perform in the cow-cutting and trail-riding events."

She wanted to leap at the chance to see him ride again but swallowed the impossible thought before she spoke. "I'd like to, but the shop is open on Saturdays."

"Not during the festival. Everything in Potter Creek closes down. It's like a ghost town. All the action's in Manhattan for the weekend."

"Are you sure? I wouldn't want to—"

"Ask Aunt Martha. She'll tell you."

Arnie tooted the van horn impatiently.

Daniel touched the brim of his hat in a casual salute. "Week from Saturday. I'll pick you up bright and early at six."

Her eyes widened. "In the morning?"

"You got it, Goldilocks. April's an early riser. I need to get her over to Manhattan in time for her to get used to the rodeo ring."

With that, he sauntered out to the van, his swagger ever-present. Once again he'd left Melinda slack-jawed and unsettled. He'd asked her for a date? And she'd accepted?

Why on earth had she done that?

Her heart squeezed as a shimmer of anticipation slid down her spine. She knew exactly why she'd said yes.

She was psychologically unable to resist Daniel O'Brien. Which made her some kind of fool.

She finished straightening the shop, turned the sign on the door to Closed and made her way to Aunt Martha's house. Her whole body ached with fatigue. But it was a good feeling of being tired. For the first time since she arrived in Potter Creek, she truly felt optimistic that she could make a success of Aunt Martha's Knitting and Notions.

Thanks to Daniel O'Brien.

From deep inside, she heard the voice of her

conscience. *"Don't get too cocky, Melinda Sue. You know you don't deserve success. Or happiness."*

She'd driven her husband away to his death and let her child die. God would never forgive either of those sins.

Chapter Seven

❧

Daniel bedded the horses down for the night and stepped out of the barn.

He tucked his fingertips in his hip pockets and looked up. In the west, the sky was a light blue, the same color as Mindy's eyes. Above him the stars had begun to shine in the darker sky. The heat of the day still hung in the air, and a faint breeze carried the lush scents of the prairie grassland.

If Daniel hadn't almost killed Arnie when he drove them off the road into a ditch, Daniel probably would have been dead by now. Back then, he'd been living hard and fast. Taking risks. Angry at his old man. And himself.

The accident had knocked some sense into him. His guilt had been like being gored by an enraged bull every morning when he woke up, every night until he went to bed. Dreams of that crash, a mammoth boulder coming toward the windshield at ninety miles an hour, the sudden stop, glass shattering, haunted him. He'd wake up screaming.

He still carried the scars from that night. Arnie's scars went much deeper.

Then Arnie had forgiven him. He'd insisted Daniel talk to Pastor Redmond. To stop the nightmares, the reverend told him, Daniel had to forgive himself and ask for God's help.

That hadn't been easy. He'd spent a lot of his waking hours praying. Finally, the Lord had lifted the burden from his shoulders.

Drawing in the lush scents traveling on the invisible currents of night air, he sent up a prayer. "Thank You, God, for giving me a second chance. Stand by me and give me strength. Help me to reflect Your goodness and to accept those things I can't change. Amen."

He closed his eyes for a moment, released a long breath, then headed into the house. He wondered if he had a second chance with Mindy or if that was one of those things he couldn't change.

All the doors and windows were open to catch a breath of air. Arnie was in the kitchen, his laptop open on the oak table where they'd eaten almost every meal since they were kids. As usual, Sheila lay sprawled on the floor beside him, her tongue lolling out. She opened one eye, identified Daniel as harmless and went back to sleep.

"What're you up to?" Daniel pulled out a chair and straddled it.

"Just messing around."

"You want a soda or something?"

"No, I'm good." Arnie hadn't bothered to look up from the computer screen.

Daniel frowned. His brother wasn't really usually so tight-lipped.

Sitting back in his chair, Arnie ran the fingers of both of his hands through his hair. "Seeing you with Mindy and not able to take your eyes off her started me thinking."

Daniel bristled. "I don't stare at her like that."

"I was thinking that someday you're going to get married."

"Hey, bro, you're going way too fast for me." He held up a hand in an effort to shut down the idea of marriage.

Arnie grunted. "So I started looking on the internet for house plans suitable for a paraplegic like me."

"What're you talkin' about? This is your house as much as it is mine. The whole downstairs is totally accessible. Everything you need is right here." Shoving up out of his chair, Daniel walked around the table to take a look at the computer screen. He peered over his brother's shoulder and frowned.

Sheila stood and stretched, then sank to the floor again while Daniel studied the one-story floor plan on the screen. Three bedrooms, two baths, extra-wide doors to accommodate a wheelchair. Ramps at both doors.

"You'd never have to move, Arnie. Even if I did get married—and I'm not seeing that happening anytime soon." Although the idea had more appeal now than it might have a couple of weeks ago. "We're brothers. We come as a package deal, the two of us."

Arnie looked up at him and narrowed his eyes. "We're not attached at the hip and three's a crowd. Besides, what if I'm the one who gets married first?"

Daniel hadn't considered that possibility. Since the accident, Arnie hadn't dated anyone, although a few women had expressed an interest. So far as Daniel knew, his brother had turned them all down.

"Hey, have you been seeing some girl on the sly?"

Arnie's brittle laugh held little humor. "That sounds like wishful thinking to me."

"Come on, Arnie. You have a lot to offer a woman. You own half the ranch, got a great sense of humor. You're good-looking. You've never given any woman half a chance to get to know you."

"I did once, remember?" In an abrupt motion, he flicked off the computer and shut the cover. "I'm a cripple. End of story."

He put the computer in his lap, backed away from the table and wheeled himself out of the kitchen. Sheila scrambled to catch up with him.

Like a sudden rock slide, guilt for what he'd done to his brother rolled over Daniel and pummeled him with the bruising weight of boulders.

He stayed where he was, staring at the scratch he'd carved into the table when he'd been about nine years old. His old man, drunk as usual, had walloped him good for that. Daniel hadn't cried. Not a whimper. But when it was over and he went up to his room, he found Arnie waiting for him, his face tear-streaked.

A muscle ticked in his jaw. Tears that he'd never shed clogged his throat.

In more ways than he could name, he owed Arnie his life. He'd been slow to pay up, but he was trying. Every day. With his very last breath, he'd still be trying.

He'd make any sacrifice necessary to pay back the debt he owed his brother.

First thing Wednesday morning, Melinda went out to get the newspaper. She brought the paper back into Martha's house and sat down at the kitchen table.

The lead story was about a ground-breaking for a new shopping development between Potter Creek and Manhattan. Officials touted the growth of the community as the reason for increased retail space.

"Great, I hope no one decides to open a knitting shop," she mumbled as she turned the page in search of a story about her grand reopening. She didn't need the competition.

She found the article above the fold on page three, including a photo of the outside of Aunt Martha's Knitting and Notions.

"Good morning, dear." The clunk-clunk of her walker announced Martha's arrival. "You're up early."

"Wanted to see what the *Courier* had to say about the shop." The story reported Melinda's enthusiasm for knitting, the shop's good-if-small selection of yarns and that, neat and clean, Aunt Martha's Knitting and Notions was a pleasant shop to visit. Martha's delight that her grandniece had reopened the shop ended the article. In a sidebar, she'd listed the classes Melinda offered.

Leaning back, Melinda blew out a breath. "It's all there. Even a few quotes she overheard when I was talking to a couple of customers. She quoted you, too."

"Oh, good. Let me see what it says." Setting her walker aside, Martha sat down and put her glasses on. Melinda handed her the paper folded to the article, then got up to put the coffee on and fix breakfast.

"Looks like Amy did a good job of reporting," Martha said.

"I just hope the article attracts some customers." The notice in the Saturday paper had been small, printed next to the ad Melinda had purchased on page five. Neither had produced a big run on the store. Maybe she ought to try an ad in the Bozeman paper. That had a lot bigger circulation but would be more expensive.

"I wouldn't worry about it, dear. After the success of your class yesterday, I'm sure the word will spread quickly."

Melinda hoped so.

After breakfast, Melinda dressed and walked the short distance to the shop. She switched the sign on the door to Open and prepared for a long, quiet day. She had a stock of off-white wool-mix yarn that would make a nice sweater for Daniel, contrasting with his sun-burnished complexion and dark hair. She'd call it a thank-you for all he'd done for her.

She did, after all, need a project to work on during the slow times in the shop. So far, there'd been a lot of those.

To her surprise, a woman opened the door and stepped inside, setting the tiny wind chimes over the door in motion. Her bright red hair looked familiar.

"Hello," the woman said. "I'm Jayne, Becca's mother. You must be Melinda."

Instantly she saw the family resemblance. Not only did they have the same red hair and freckles, their heart-shaped faces were almost identical. "Yes, I'm Melinda. Your daughter's a sweet girl."

Jayne flashed a quick smile of pride. "Thank you, I think so, too. She was full of talk last night at dinner about you and your shop and the knitting project the youngsters are working on."

"Once they get started, I think the project will be fun for them. Do you knit, Mrs. Audis?"

She glanced around the shop. "I'm afraid not. I'm a quilter. A few of us get together once a week or so to quilt. And gossip, I admit." Her self-conscious laugh came out as a high-pitched titter. "Please call me Jayne. When someone says Mrs. Audis, I always think they're talking about my mother-in-law."

Melinda could relate to that. Adele Spencer had been a formidable woman who always knew what was best for her son Joe. "Perhaps someday I'll be able to convert you to knitting."

"Entirely possible, particularly if Becca gets more involved with knitting," she agreed. "Today, though, I dropped by to talk to you about the Community Church's craft fair we host during the fall."

Her interest piqued, Melinda's brows lifted. "Oh?"

"It's a fairly large affair. We draw craftspeople from

a wide area who sell their products during the two-day event. We have artists and woodworkers, quilters, of course, and a lovely young lady who does sculptures. Some stained glass is shown. Almost every craft you can name. I'm the chairperson this year, and I thought you might like to have a booth where your knitters can show off their wares."

"That sounds like a good idea." It would be even better if she actually had some customers who did high-quality knitting.

"It would be nice publicity for your shop."

"True," Melinda agreed.

"I also thought, because you attend the church, you'd be willing to serve on the committee. That way there'd be no charge for the shop's booth."

"I'm, um, so new in town." Something tightened in Melinda's stomach. She only attended church because Martha insisted on going every Sunday.

She glanced away from Jayne and picked up a stray paper clip from the counter, unbending it.

"How long you've lived here doesn't matter," Jayne said. "What we need are willing hands to help plan and organize the event." She gestured around the store. "I can already tell you're great at organizing. The shop is beautifully set up. And anyone who can handle nearly a dozen teenagers has more patience and strength of character than I do."

"We've only had one class," Melinda pointed out, tossing the straightened paper clip in the trash. "You might want to withhold judgment about that for a while."

Jane tittered again, a happy sound like a little bird inviting a friend to play. "Here, let me give you my phone number." She found a piece of paper and a pen in her purse. "Our next committee meeting is Thursday evening at seven in the community room at church. We'd love to have you drop by. You don't have to make a commitment, but you would have a chance to meet everyone. It's a nice group of folks."

Taking the slip of paper from Jayne, Melinda studied the phone number. If she was going to stay in Potter Creek indefinitely, she did need to sink some roots into the community. And make friends.

"The church youth group is coming again tomorrow. After that I'll have to fix dinner for Aunt Martha, but I'll try to drop by." She hoped God wouldn't mind her audacity.

Later in the day, two women entered the shop. They browsed and chatted about knitting something for Susie, whoever she was, and a grandchild. They didn't buy anything, but Melinda hoped they'd come back another day.

On Thursday, three women came in. One actually bought a new yarn winder. Not a great morning at the cash register, but at least people were becoming aware the shop was open again.

Melinda closed the shop for the lunch hour to check on Aunt Martha and fix her something to eat. Aunt Martha still wasn't too steady on her feet, so preparing a meal at the kitchen counter was beyond her. Melinda had gotten her a cell phone so she could call her at the shop or call 9-1-1 if necessary.

Even so, she worried about her aunt Martha. Fortunately, almost every day one of her friends stopped by to visit. Melinda envied the longtime friendships Martha had established over the years.

Right at three o'clock, Grace Staples popped into the shop. "I hope I'm not too early." Wearing shorts, a tank top and sandals, she looked ready to take on the sweltering heat of summer.

"Not at all. Your timing is perfect." Her eagerness was infectious even for Melinda.

"My mom said my sister is having a boy, so I guess I have to use blue yarn for his cap."

"Not necessarily. Let's look through some patterns first."

Sitting down at the table, Grace flipped through a couple of pattern books. She chose an easy two-needle baby hat that took only one ball of angora-blend yarn.

"Maybe if the hat turns out okay, I can make him a sweater, too."

"Sounds perfect to me." Melinda led her to the bin of angora-mix yarn and showed her the various colors, even some variegated yarn in bright shades, including red, white and blue.

The sixteen-year-old picked up a variegated skein. "Oh, wow, that'd be so awesome. Baby blue is so last century."

Melinda nearly choked. "You might want to think about what your sister would like best. Is she the traditional sort or more chic-modern?"

Grace grinned. "Definitely chic. She subscribes to every fashion magazine that exists."

"Perfect." Melinda let the girl pick out the brightest colors she wanted, then showed her the needles that would work best.

Melinda held the skein while Grace rolled the ball. Rolling yarn with a friend was a bonding experience and conversation came easily. Grace told her about school and her dream of being a nurse. Melinda told her about growing up in Pittsburgh and big-city living.

Soon they were casting on the first row of stitches.

Melinda wasn't sure how much time had passed when she heard the tinkling wind chimes over the door announce a visitor.

With a smile on her face, and expecting to see one of the youngsters from the church group or even Daniel, she turned to see who had arrived.

Her smile melted away like heated candle wax. Her stomach dipped somewhere toward her toes. A moment later, it bounced back and she straightened her shoulders. She chided herself for the wave of jealousy and insecurity that had washed through her. Smothering her childish reaction, she forced a smile.

Chapter Eight

"Hello, Ivy. What can I do for you?" Melinda asked in a welcoming voice.

Wearing a summery dress, Ivy sauntered in with plenty of hip movement and gave the shop a cursory look. "I thought I'd sign up for your knitting class."

Melinda touched Grace's arm. "You go ahead and finish casting on." She stood to meet Ivy. "I'm glad you decided to give knitting a try. The church youth group has pretty well filled up my Tuesday and Thursday afternoon classes for now, but if there's another time that would be good for you, I'm sure we can work something out."

The young woman took a pose, thrusting her hip out and planting her fist. "Really? I can't see any reason why I can't be part of the class, too. After all, I am a member of the church."

Which had nothing to do with the class already being too large to easily manage. "You're certainly welcome to join in, if that's what you'd like. They've decided to make a lap robe for a wounded soldier as a service project."

Ivy wrinkled her nose. "Whatever."

"If you'd like to knit something else, like a scarf, I'll try to help you. But I won't be able to give you as much individual attention as I'd like to with someone new to knitting."

Ivy strolled with feigned nonchalance over to Grace. "That doesn't look like a lap robe to me."

"My sister's expecting," Grace explained to Ivy, who was probably four or five years her senior. "I'm making a hat for the baby."

"How sweet." Her words dripped with sarcasm like bitter chocolate over a dish of ice cream.

"I'm helping Grace individually because she already knows how to knit and she's helping me with the class."

"Gracey always has been a teacher's pet, haven't you?"

Color rose on Grace's cheeks but she didn't respond.

The door opened. Laughing, Becca and a friend stepped inside. They came to a halt when they saw Ivy.

"Hey, Ivy," Becca said. She went to retrieve the class's box of yarn and needles on the back shelf while her friend sat down next to Grace.

"Becca, you won't mind if I join the class, will you?" Ivy asked in a sugar-sweet voice.

Becca glanced at Melinda. "It's not up to me."

"As I said, Ivy, you're welcome to stay, if that's what

you want." She had the distinct impression that Ivy had something in mind other than knitting, namely making points with Daniel O'Brien. "There is a charge for the yarn and needles"

"No problem." The young woman plucked some money from her pocket. Mindy made change.

When the door opened a minute or two later, Ivy pasted on a bright smile. Melinda turned to see who had arrived and found Daniel striding into the shop behind his brother's wheelchair.

Unable to stop herself, her welcoming smile mirrored Ivy's and probably was equally foolish.

"Hey, gang," he said. "Where is everybody?"

"Dwayne has a dentist appointment," Becca told him. "Everybody else is coming, I think."

"Good." He spotted Ivy and gave her a slow look. "You here to make lap robes for Wounded Warriors?"

Turning slightly sideways, she flicked her long hair behind her shoulder and curled her lips into a flirtatious smile. "Sure. Why not? They deserve our support, right?"

Gritting her teeth, Melinda turned away to greet Arnie. "He talked you into coming back, I see."

A teasing gleam sparked in his eyes. "Anything to help my brother's love life along."

Melinda choked and coughed, suddenly unable to catch her breath.

Barking a boisterous laugh, Arnie wheeled past her to his place at the back table.

Pulling herself together as the rest of the group

arrived, Melinda vowed not to let Arnie's words—or Ivy's presence—disrupt the class.

The teenagers seemed more subdued today than they had been during the first class. There was less shoving and jostling and more whispered conversations. Melinda caught several of the youngsters eyeing Ivy, which made her curious about the young woman's reputation in town. The high schoolers didn't ignore her, but they weren't very cordial, either. Perhaps it was simply the age gap. Fifteen-, sixteen- and seventeen-year-olds versus a woman who looked to be in her early twenties.

"All right, everyone, let's get back to casting on," she announced. "Grace, would you help Ivy roll a ball of the yarn she'll need for the lap robe? If that's what you want to do, Ivy."

Ivy did a fair imitation of a queenly wave of dismissal. "Whatever."

Melinda picked up her needles and yarn. "For the lap robes, we're going to make ten-inch squares, so I want you to pull a little more than ten inches off your ball of yarn."

"Have you got a ruler?" a girl asked.

"Make it as long as Pete's nose," a boy responded to a round of guffaws from his friends.

"I'm still rolling my yarn," Ivy complained.

"I'm sure you'll be able to catch up," Melinda assured her.

Once everyone except Ivy was ready, Melinda demonstrated how to hold their needles and the yarn. Patti said she was left-handed; Melinda encouraged her to try first right-handed. If that didn't work, she could reverse the instructions.

"I want you all to cast on ten stitches," Melinda said. "As we go along, some of you will find you enjoy knitting and it goes fast for you. If so, you may want to knit more than one square. That way we can make up two or three lap robes for our wounded warriors."

Moving around the table, Melinda checked each youngster, making sure the stitches were neither too loose nor too tight. Some of the students were clearly more coordinated or used to working with their hands than others.

When she got to Daniel, she discovered he'd inadvertently created a granny knot instead of a slip knot and had pulled it tight. Rather than trying to undo the knot, she used her scissors to snip the yarn and started over.

Pulling off another length of yarn, she showed him how to hold his needles again and the way to drape the yarn over and under his fingers to create the proper tension. His fingers were long and slightly rough to the touch. His warm breath on her cheek fluttered a few strands of her hair. She tried not to inhale his masculine scent but failed.

"Guess I'm not exactly an A student yet," he said.

"It takes practice." The husky sound of her voice sounded unfamiliar to her own ears.

"Ms. Spencer, can you help me, please?"

Instinctively, Melinda pulled back from Daniel and glanced toward Ivy. The girl's saccharine smile looked as innocent as a rattler about to strike.

"Grace will show you, Ivy." She moved on to Arnie, who seemed to be doing fine.

When everyone had cast on the first row, she showed them how to knit the next. Purl would follow that, reversing the way the needle entered the stitches. Again she checked each student's progress, but whenever she got within arm's length of Daniel, Ivy demanded her attention for one thing or another. She noted Daniel rarely if ever glanced in Ivy's direction or gave any indication that he was particularly aware of her presence.

Melinda began to feel sorry for the young woman. She either was deluded thinking Daniel returned her interest or she had a childish crush on the man. Melinda could understand the latter. But if that were the case, it would be a kindness if Daniel let her down easily.

By the time the class ended, Melinda was feeling the strain of Ivy's eagle eye on her constantly just waiting to pounce on any misstep she might make with Daniel.

After the others had left, Daniel lingered. So did Ivy.

"Tonight's special at the diner is pot roast," Ivy announced. "Why don't you and Arnie come in for supper?"

"Can't tonight, Ivy. You go on now. I've got to talk to Melinda for a minute."

With a pouty flick of her hair, Ivy whirled and flounced out the door.

Melinda blew out a relieved sigh. "I know it's none of my business, but is there something going on between you and Ivy?"

"Not really." He glanced out the door where Ivy had

just made her dramatic exit. "A couple of months ago I was kind of teasing with her at the diner. I think she got the wrong idea. She's too young for me and she's too desperate, I guess you could say." He returned his attention to Melinda. "Her mother died when she was pretty young, her dad isn't a real warm kind of guy. I think Ivy is anxious to get away from him, but he keeps her on a tight leash."

"So she sets her sights on a handsome cowboy as a way out?"

"Something like that." He lifted his broad shoulders in a casual don't-blame-me shrug. "As I hear it, I'm not the first guy she's thought would be her ticket out of Potter Creek."

"How sad." Melinda's growing sympathy for Ivy hadn't been misplaced, which didn't make dealing with her any easier. "I think you ought to let her know how you feel."

"I've tried. It doesn't seem to do much good. She's fixated on me."

Once upon a time, Melinda had been, too.

He pulled a check from his shirt pocket. "If you've got that invoice ready, I can pay you for the kids' yarn and supplies."

She walked behind the counter, opened the register and retrieved the invoice she'd prepared.

Taking the invoice, Daniel glanced at the total and filled out the check. "You're a good teacher, Mindy."

Heat warmed her cheeks. Good teacher or not, having Daniel in the class was an anxiety-producing element she wished she didn't have to repeat.

After closing up the shop, Melinda fixed Aunt Martha a quick dinner of chicken breast and wild rice.

"I hate to leave you all alone tonight because you've been alone all day," Melinda said as she was hurriedly cleaning up the dishes.

"Oh, don't worry about me, dear. Sylvia Goodsend's daughter brought her over this afternoon and purely wore me out with all of her gossip."

"You're sure you'll be all right?"

"I've lived alone most of my life, dear. One more night alone won't bother me."

A pang of grief punched Melinda in her midsection. Grief for the loss of Jason and for Joe. And grief for all Aunt Martha had missed by remaining single. She'd never understood why Martha had never married. She'd seen snapshots of her as a young woman; she'd been quite attractive.

"I promise I won't be late."

"Enjoy yourself, dear. It's good for you to get out a little."

Melinda picked up a shawl made of Kid Merino and Waikiki yarns and draped it around her shoulders. Because she was in the knitting business, she liked to show off the garments she'd made and the rose-colored stole flattered her complexion.

A few minutes late for the meeting, Melinda found a dozen people, two of them men, already gathered around a long table in the church community room. She spotted Jayne Audis, who waved her over.

"I'm so glad you came, Melinda."

"Sorry I'm late."

"Not a problem. We're just getting started." Jayne introduced her to the committee members. The two men and most of the women were well over fifty. Two of the women appeared to be in their thirties, one a mother of triplets, according to Jayne's introduction.

"I don't think I have any friends who knit these days," said one of the older women. "Several do needlepoint, but they have to order their supplies online or drive to Bozeman."

"As soon as I get the shop up and on a solid footing, I'm hoping to expand to include needlepoint," Melinda said. "We did a lot of needlepoint business at the shop where I worked in Pittsburgh."

"Oh, they'd like that. None of us like to drive to Bozeman if we can help it. All that traffic, you know. And buying online means shipping fees run up the expense of a project." She nodded to herself. "I'll tell them about your shop. They'll probably drop in to see you."

Melinda smiled. "I'd love to meet them." She realized if she couldn't compete with Bozeman shops or the internet, she'd lose business. She couldn't afford to do that. So when Jayne suggested she check out the competition in Bozeman, she readily agreed.

Chapter Nine

The following morning, Daniel woke up thinking about Melinda and wanting to go into town to see her. She hadn't really thought he had something going on with Ivy, had she? That was crazy.

Then again, maybe it meant she was a tiny bit jealous.

As he finished shaving, he grinned at his reflection in the mirror. He could live with that.

But not today. He had to get out to the north pasture to change the oil in the old windmill or the gears would freeze up on him. Thirsty cattle didn't do well in a Montana summer.

Climbing up the windmill to handle repairs was one of the few things around the ranch Arnie couldn't manage. Not that he wouldn't try. He was forever trying to prove he wasn't the cripple he called himself.

He jogged down the stairs and into the kitchen. Arnie had the coffee on, and Daniel poured himself a mugful.

"What's on the schedule for today?" Arnie asked.

"Fixing the windmill. When we moved the herd out there, it was groaning like it was on its last legs."

Arnie looked at him over the top of his mug. "I thought you might go into town, pay Mindy a visit."

"Nope." Daniel dropped two slices of bread into the toaster. "No need. I'll see her at church on Sunday."

"That's no way to court a lady."

Turning, Daniel leaned back against the counter and crossed his arms in front of him. "What's with you lately? You trying to play matchmaker? You ever think maybe I don't want to get married?"

"Then you'd be a fool, bro." He wheeled back from the table and pushed himself out of the room with angry strokes, like a racer determined to reach the finish line first.

The toast popped up, but Daniel didn't move. Something bad was eating at his brother. Could Arnie have his eye on Mindy, too? Or was his anger because Daniel had put him in that wheelchair and now he was afraid life was passing him by?

Daniel thought his brother had gotten past the depression that had plagued him after the accident.

A moment later, Daniel heard the clank of Arnie's weight-lifting equipment. That was how his brother coped when things got tough. By the time he built up a good sweat, his mood would improve. Usually.

He plucked the toast from the toaster and spread on some butter. Whatever Arnie's problem was, Daniel hoped he could work it out without doing himself too much damage.

* * *

Melinda shook her head. "Aunt Martha, I can't leave you to run the shop alone."

"I've been running the shop alone for years, dear."

"That was *before* you had the stroke." They'd been eating breakfast when Melinda told her aunt about visiting the knitting shop in Bozeman. Despite her best efforts, she hadn't been able to figure out how to be in two places at once, Bozeman and Aunt Martha's Knitting and Notions, and she didn't want to close the shop for half a day.

"Oh, fiddles and scallywags." She waved her hand at an imaginary fly. "You won't be gone but a few hours. If you can get me to the shop, I can sit there as well as I can sit here at home."

Knowing her aunt could be stubborn when she set her mind on something, Melinda struggled to find a suitable alternative. "Could you get a friend to come sit with you?"

Blinking, Martha considered the idea. "I'm not sure. Maybe Rose could come over for a bit. Or Abbie from church."

"Why don't you call them while I clean up the kitchen and get dressed." She picked up their cereal bowls and carried them to the sink.

Using her walker, Martha went into the living room where the phone extension sat next to her favorite chair. She refused to use the cell phone Melinda had given her for anything other than an emergency, which thankfully hadn't happened so far.

As Melinda washed their breakfast dishes, she could

hear Martha on the phone. Sometimes she thought her aunt knew every resident of Potter Creek and their entire personal history.

With a familiar pang of remorse, she felt fortunate no one in town knew her history or her failures. In Potter Creek, she wasn't the constant recipient of sympathy or the scathing condemnation that her in-laws had heaped on her.

Returning to the kitchen, Martha said, "Rose has a doctor's appointment this morning and you know how hard those are to change. But Abbie said she'd be happy to come visit. She'll meet us at the shop about ten."

Satisfied with Martha's solution, Melinda dressed in slacks and a lightweight, pale blue blouse. Wanting to be a credible professional when she faced her competition, she switched to a felted clutch purse made of wool yarn with an acrylic and cotton core. The pastel colors looked both summery and cool.

After getting Martha and her friend Abbie settled at the shop, Melinda drove to Bozeman, about a half hour away. Knitting & Needles was located in a strip shopping center that was anchored by a large chain grocery store. Ample parking made for easy access and convenience.

Carrying a handful of flyers for the craft fair, Melinda stepped into the shop. Well-lit with an open feeling, the store had twice the square footage as Aunt Martha's shop. Fully a quarter of the space was dedicated to needlepoint supplies with several beautifully done samples on display.

Melinda developed an instant case of envy. How

could she ever compete with the array of merchandise Knitting & Needles carried?

Several women were sitting at a table in the back of the shop, working on their needlepoint projects and chatting among themselves.

Melinda wandered over to the yarn bins and checked their prices. Despite a larger variety to choose from than she carried, the prices were about what she was charging for comparable merchandise. That, at least, was encouraging. Knitting & Needles wasn't selling at a discount she wouldn't be able to meet.

"Hello. May I help you?"

Turning, Melinda smiled at the woman who had approached her. Older than Melinda by a decade or more, she wore her blond hair piled on top of her head in studied disarray. Reading glasses dangled around her neck on a gold chain.

"I was looking for the owner or the manager," Melinda said.

"I'm Jenny Fortune, one of the co-owners. What can I do for you?"

Melinda introduced herself. "I'm from Potter Creek. Our church is going to host our annual craft fair again this fall." She handed Jenny one of the flyers. "We're hoping either your shop or some of your ladies will want to rent a booth and show off their projects."

Lifting her glasses to her eyes without actually putting them on, Jenny studied the flyer. "Oh, yes, several of our ladies had a booth last year. They did quite well selling some items. Baby blankets and booties were the most popular."

Nodding knowingly, Melinda said, "Grandmothers can't resist, can they?"

Jenny chuckled. "How well I know that." She took the rest of the flyers and promised to make them available to her clientele.

After Melinda explained that she was now managing Aunt Martha's shop in Potter Creek, Jenny gave her a brief tour of the store. She dutifully admired the quality and variety of the merchandise while mentally noting what changes she'd have to make at Aunt Martha's Knitting and Notions to be competitive.

By the time she got back into her car, Melinda had decided if Aunt Martha's was to survive, she'd have to start carrying needlepoint merchandise immediately. That meant she'd have to get a loan and she was already in debt to Daniel. She couldn't ask him to underwrite her business expansion. She'd have to try for a bank loan and go through whatever hoops they demanded.

Given her painful experience of declaring bankruptcy to wipe out her enormous medical debts, simply thinking about asking for a loan made sweat bead her forehead and her mouth go dry.

Sunday morning as Melinda pushed Aunt Martha in her wheelchair up the walkway to church, Daniel fell in step beside them.

"Good morning, ladies. You're both looking lovely this morning."

Melinda bit her lip and squeezed the handles of Martha's wheelchair more tightly. How could Daniel appear so relaxed and at ease when she tensed like a length of yarn stretched and pulled too tight every time he showed up?

"Why, thank you, Daniel." Martha laughed and took his hand. "A lady always enjoys hearing that from a gentleman."

"It's only the truth, Aunt Martha." He released her hand. "Here, let me push her chair," he said to Melinda.

"No, I've got it. Don't you have to usher or greet people or something?"

"Nope, not today." He eased her out of the way and took over behind the wheelchair. "I don't have any duties at all."

"Oh, good," Martha said. "Then you can sit with us this morning."

"No, he doesn't want to—"

"I'd love to." He shot Melinda his patented smile that all but made her toes curl.

She edged away from him and the wheelchair, reminding herself that she was walking into the house of God.

"The high school group is having a picnic at the river this evening," he said. "Hot dogs. Bonfire. Marshmallows. Singing. The whole bit. But one of the chaperones had to cancel. I'm hoping you can fill in for her."

Her staccato refusal came out as a sharp note.

"You'd have fun, dear," Martha said. "Don't worry about me."

Melinda rolled her eyes. Going to Riverside Park with Daniel had started her downfall ten years ago. She didn't want a repeat of that experience.

The greeter at the door handed each of them a program with a welcoming smile.

"If we don't have enough chaperones, the kids can't go." Lowering his voice, Daniel wheeled Martha down the side aisle. "The church has rules about that. The kids have been planning this picnic for weeks."

Guilt kicked her in her soft heart. Or perhaps it was her need for a do-over and to get it right this time. "I really should stay home with Martha."

He parked Martha at the end of a pew.

"Go and have some fun, dear. I'll watch one of those reality shows where everyone makes a fool of themselves."

Daniel stepped back so Melinda could enter the pew first. His dark eyes challenged her to refuse his invitation. Refuse to chaperone the kids.

Her smarter self crumbled under his penetrating gaze and she wimped out. She gave a quick nod and brushed past him, entering the pew wondering what she was getting herself into.

Riverside Park was much as she remembered it. Picnic tables constructed of concrete. Fire pit circles made of native stone. Willow trees lining the river upstream from the swimming beach. Slow-moving water meandering downstream, and the cliffs her friend Ellie James and the boys had climbed was on the far shore.

She sat at a picnic table while the kids got the fire going under the supervision of Tracy and Paul Chvostal, the other chaperones, who were parents of two of the teenagers in the group. She heard a nearby radio playing country-and-western music. Closing her eyes, she remembered how it had been ten years ago.

Laughing with Daniel and his friends while they played catch with a Frisbee.

Perched on Daniel's shoulders in the water while trying to topple another girl sitting on her boyfriend's shoulders, arm wrestling her as best she could.

Melinda's lips curved as she recalled how she'd almost sunk Daniel when she'd become unbalanced and wouldn't let him go.

"You must be thinking of something pretty nice."

She opened her eyes to look up at Daniel, who was standing in front of her. In the twilight, his face was shadowed, the muted light softening the hard angles of his cheekbones and firm jaw.

She couldn't tell him, wouldn't remind him of the past. Didn't want him remembering, too.

With a force of willpower, she changed the direction of her thoughts. "Whatever happened to DeeDee Pickens?"

He blinked several times in rapid succession. "Dee-Dee? I don't remember—"

"You don't remember the girl you gave a ring to?"

Scratching the edge of his jaw, he shook his head. "I don't know what you're talking about. I've never given any girl a ring."

His expression looked innocent, but how could that be? "She told me... She showed me the ring. It wasn't a diamond. Something pink. She was a cheerleader at school." Bubbly personality, all cute and feminine with a mean streak a half-mile wide.

"Oh! You mean Delores Pickens. I never gave her anything, Mindy. She was always telling her friends how we were going to get married. I wasn't interested in marrying anybody. She knew that. She just wanted to trap me. It didn't work."

Lowering her head, she rubbed her left hand over her chest as though she could erase the ache that bloomed there. "She was the reason… She's why I left Potter Creek in such a hurry. I thought—"

He planted one booted foot on the bench next to her and cupped her chin, forcing her to look up. "She lied, Mindy. We went out a couple of times, but I never gave her a ring. I swear it."

She swallowed hard. Had she misjudged Daniel all these years? Been so stupid as to believe a lie told by a jealous girl who wanted to run her out of town?

"I believe you." The encroaching darkness absorbed her whispered words and wrapped itself around the two of them. The laughter from the fire ring seemed distant, another world. "I'm sorry."

"I'm sorry, too."

"Hey, you two!" Paul shouted from the fire ring, shattering the moment. "Time to cook your hot dogs."

Daniel hesitated, then glanced over his shoulder. "We're coming."

Lunging to her feet, Melinda stepped away from him. She struggled to find something to say, anything that would not reveal the yearning she felt. "I'm going to expand the shop to include needlepoint."

"Oh?" He turned toward the fire ring. "I thought you were going to wait until the knitting business was stable."

"I was until I visited the knitting shop in Bozeman. I have to be competitive with them if I'm going to have any chance to succeed." As they walked, she quickly told him about Knitting & Needles, its size and the merchandise it carried.

"That's going to take a lot of cash," he pointed out.

"I'm going to ask the bank for a loan, big enough so I can pay you back and have enough to build up the needlepoint side of the business."

His slid his fingertips into his back pockets. "There's no hurry to pay me back."

"But I want to. With a bank loan, I can spread out the payments over several years. It'll all work out." She hoped.

"You'll have to write up a business plan. The bank won't loan you money unless they know what you're going to do with it."

A business plan? She could do that. "No problem."

"They'll check your credit."

Ouch! They'd find out about her bankruptcy. "Except for my own credit card, you're the only person I owe money to."

"Don't tell 'em about me. We don't have anything in writing. You don't want my loan to affect your credit."

Of course not. She had bigger problems than his thousand-dollar loan. Like the bankruptcy she'd hated to file. And now having to borrow money to get the shop running.

Belatedly, Melinda realized she hadn't been doing a very good job of chaperoning the kids. Talk about being easily distracted when Daniel was around.

She smiled to herself. *He hadn't given DeeDee a ring!*

All those years of feeling he had betrayed her, she'd been wrong. At least as far as DeeDee was concerned.

Which didn't mean he'd been an angel in cowboy boots, she reminded herself. She still would have had to return to Pittsburgh and leave her summer romance behind. But it wouldn't have hurt so much.

With a long-handled fork in hand, she stabbed a hotdog and squeezed in between Becca and Grace, who were sitting on the stone fire ring.

"How long do you cook these things?" she asked.

"Depends on whether you like them burned to charcoal or not," Grace responded.

"I think *not* would be my choice."

"The guys all think eating charcoal is macho," Becca commented.

"Bet they'd eat snips and snails and puppy dog tails, too, if they thought it would impress the girls," Melinda said, quoting the old poem about what boys are made of.

Both girls giggled. "I don't even know what a snip is," Becca said.

"Oh, I think that's little bits of string or rocks or

shells," Melinda told them. "Anything little boys can and do stick in their mouths."

Their giggles turned into gales of laughter, Melinda joining in the fun.

Melinda glanced across the fire ring. Daniel caught her eye and volleyed a smile back that smacked into her chest with life-changing force. Her good intentions wavered. Her heart squeezed tight.

With all of her shortcomings, her transgressions against those she had loved, did she dare allow herself to dream again?

Chapter Ten

During the next few days, Melinda spent every spare moment working up a business plan to expand Aunt Martha's shop to carry needlepoint merchandise.

She checked catalogs and contacted wholesalers about prices. She estimated sales volume, perhaps too optimistically, and the cost of an advertising blitz. She drew sketches of how she would rearrange the current bins and merchandise to add new ones. She created a spreadsheet with so many columns that her head spun and she nearly went cross-eyed.

By Friday she was ready to present her business plan to the local branch manager of Montana Ranchers and Merchants Bank. She called for an appointment and arranged to meet him when the shop was closed during her lunch hour.

When she stepped inside the bank, she felt as though she'd stepped back in time. A polished mahogany counter stretched the length of the room. The two tellers behind the counter wore white shirts with black string ties, green visors and matching cuff protectors. In front of the counter there were two ornate spittoons, which she sincerely hoped were for trash and not their originally intended purpose.

Richard Connolly, the bank manager, sat off to the side at a large desk. He, too, wore a white shirt and string tie with silver tips, but without the visor and cuff protectors. The presence of a computer reassured Melinda that she was still in the twenty-first century.

She introduced herself. Giving her a professional smile, Mr. Connolly stepped around his desk to shake her hand.

"A belated welcome to Potter Creek, Ms. Spencer." He gestured to the leather chairs in front of his desk. "How is your aunt these days?"

"Her recovery is going well, thank you. She's feeling strong and getting around better than she had initially." Physical therapy was working wonders, for which Melinda was grateful.

Once Melinda was seated, Mr. Connolly returned to his seat behind his imposing desk.

"Now, then, what can we do for you and Aunt Martha?"

"As you may know, I've taken over managing her knitting shop. I've upgraded the current merchandise, started some classes, which have been well-attended." Thanks to Daniel and his youth group. "However, to be competitive, I need to expand the stock to include needlepoint, which has become very popular in recent years."

She handed him a manila folder containing her business plan.

He flipped open the folder. "I have to confess I know very little about knitting and needlepoint."

She explained her vision and the need for expansion. "I'm asking for only a modest loan to buy new stock and make a few changes in the way I'll display merchandise. I estimate I'll be able to pay the loan back within five years."

"I see." He perused the business plan, then looked up. "What do you intend to use as collateral?"

"Collateral?" she echoed.

"Yes. Do you and Aunt Martha plan to guarantee the loan with either the shop or Aunt Martha's house or perhaps some property you own elsewhere?"

Melinda's heart plummeted. "Her house and shop are my aunt's only assets. I couldn't put them at risk." If, at some point, Aunt Martha had to move to a retirement home, she'd need the funds from the sale of her property.

"I see. The lack of collateral complicates matters." He leaned back in his chair and tented his fingers under his chin. A pucker of concern appeared between his brows. "We do like to support our local merchants here in Potter Creek whenever we can. Unsecured loans are a bit problematic, however."

"I assure you, I have every intention of paying back the loan."

"Of course." Pulling open a drawer in a nearby filing cabinet, he plucked out a form and slid it across the desk to her. "If you'd like to fill this out with your financial history and the shop's annual income and expenses, I'll forward the information and your request to our main office in Billings. They make the final decisions about loans."

Her heart thudded a heavy beat, one of inevitable defeat. Her shoulders threatened to slump, but she forced a pleasant smile to her lips that she knew was a lie. Her hand shook as she reached for the form that would unmask her and destroy her plans.

Potato Festival or not, Saturday morning arrived way too early. Knowing the weather would be hot, Melinda wore shorts and a T-shirt, and brought along a straw hat with a wide brim to keep the sun out of her eyes. Plus plenty of sunscreen.

When Daniel parked his truck and horse trailer in front of the house, Melinda stepped outside to greet him before he could come to the door. Her aunt was still sleeping. Melinda didn't want to wake her. She'd set out a muffin for Aunt Martha's breakfast and had made a salad for lunch, which she left in the refrigerator. To make sure her aunt would be all right, she'd arranged for one of the ladies from church to drop in on her during the afternoon.

"Morning, Goldilocks." Daniel thumbed a dressy, cream-colored Stetson farther back on his head. "You're looking especially chipper this morning."

She didn't feel it. She'd fretted all night about the loan, sure she wouldn't get it and afraid if she did she'd have to work a night job to pay the money back.

"Early morning is not my best time of day," she admitted.

He walked her around to the passenger side of the truck, opened the door and sang in a soft baritone, "'The morning light is breaking, the darkness disappears…'"

She halted abruptly, one foot on the running board. "You sing? Hymns? In the morning?"

His lips quirked into a grin. "Usually in the shower. I made an exception for you."

"Right." Shaking her head in bemusement, she pulled herself the rest of the way into the truck cab. "I gather April is in the trailer."

"She is. All washed and brushed and raring to go."

Closing the door, he jogged around to the driver's side, looking like he was raring to go, as well, in dark blue jeans and a freshly pressed, Western-cut shirt.

"This is a big day for me and April." Starting the engine, he pulled away from the curb. "Last year we lost both the trail event and cow-cutting to Charlie Moffett from Three Forks. He won't beat us this time around." Daniel lifted his chin like a boxer might taunt his opponent in the ring.

"What if you don't win?"

He glanced at her, his dark brows scrolled down above his eyes. "Then Arnie will have my hide and the bank will own half of our stock."

"You're serious?"

"As serious as a colicky horse. We've got a big loan payment coming up soon and the two events we're in have nice big purses." He gunned the truck up the entrance to the highway. "Speaking of loans, have you talked with Rich Connolly at the bank?"

Puffing out her cheeks, she blew out a breath. "I did yesterday. He's sending the forms and my business plan to Billings for approval."

"You don't sound optimistic."

"I'm not really. If they check my credit, which I assume they will, they'll find out my credit rating has tanked. I'm not exactly a good risk."

"How come?"

Wincing, shame and guilt heating her face, she looked out the window at the passing scenery—an old pickup raising a streamer of dust on a farm road, a field deep green with potato plants, a weathered barn that had seen better days. She didn't want to tell Daniel about her bankruptcy or why she'd had to take such a drastic step.

"Guess it's none of my business," he said.

"Because you loaned me more than a thousand dollars, it should be your business."

"No, don't worry about it. I know you're good for the loan."

Maybe. Business had picked up lately. Not enough to shout about yet, but enough that she felt marginally encouraged.

A few miles later, they joined a line of cars and trucks leaving the highway at the Manhattan fairgrounds exit. They passed the carnival area with its Ferris wheel and Tilt-a-Whirl and made it through heavy traffic to the rodeo arena at the far end of the complex. Daniel pulled the truck and horse trailer in line with a dozen other trailers and killed the engine.

"I'll get April out and let her stretch her legs a little before our afternoon events," Daniel said. "Then we can wander around, check out some of the booths. Arnie's here somewhere trying to win the chili cook-off."

"The chili you brought over for Aunt Martha and me was delicious."

"He's tried about sixteen new recipes since that one, including one that will turn your tonsils to charcoal."

She wrinkled her nose. "Sounds delicious."

With a laugh, Daniel got out of the truck. Melinda followed suit, dropping to the ground on the passenger side and putting on her straw hat to shade her eyes. Warm morning air heavy with the scent of dust and leather and hay rode on the sounds of friends greeting friends and the steady beat of an anvil shaping metal on metal.

A big, round O'Brien Ranch logo decorated the side of the horse trailer. Inside, April shifted her weight, rocking the trailer, and blew out a breath.

"It's all right, sweetheart." Daniel crooned in a soft, reassuring voice as he climbed into the back of the trailer. "We're here. Come on out and take a look around." He backed the horse out of the trailer.

"Oh, she is beautiful." With a gasp of delight, Melinda admired the lovely sorrel, her blond mane and tail contrasting with the darker reddish-brown of her coat. Although she wasn't an experienced judge of horse-flesh, she could tell April was a lean, well-muscled and nicely proportioned mare. "She looks like she's just back from the beauty shop where she got a color job and highlights."

Daniel boomed a deep laugh, which made April sidestep away from him. "She's all natural, Goldilocks. What you see is what you get. Just like you."

Heat rose to Melinda's cheeks and a giddy high-pitched laugh escaped her lips. "In this case, I guess it's a compliment to be compared to your horse."

He winked at her. "Come on, let's walk April around the arena, let her get used to the place." He untied April's tether and led her to the lane that had been left between parked vehicles.

Dozens of cowboys were lounging around their trucks, grooming their horses or visiting with their friends. A masculine world of loud laughter, casual bantering back and forth and rich earthy scents of hay and horses.

As they passed one cluster of men, she heard a flirtatious whistle followed by a shout. "Hey, good lookin'. I've got coffee ready whenever you're thirsty."

Melinda's cheeks heated with a blush, but she didn't turn around to see who had paid her the unwanted *compliment*.

Daniel kept on walking, as well. "Ignore these guys. Their mothers didn't teach them good manners."

As Melinda recalled, ten years ago Daniel had been the biggest flirt in Potter Creek. She suspected, despite his current good behavior, at heart he still had an eye for a pretty woman.

He stopped by groups of his friends and introduced her. The men, while courteous, tipping their hats to her, scrutinized her in a way that made her self-conscious. She didn't like being the center of attention.

A man who was grooming a well-formed buckskin shouted, "Hey, O'Brien! You bring that same nag you had last year? She doesn't have a prayer of winning this year."

Daniel whirled toward the voice and narrowed his gaze. "I'll let her speak for herself in the ring, Charlie. If I was you, I'd give Arapaho an extra ration of oats. He's gonna need it."

He tugged on April's lead and kept on walking.

"What was that all about?" Melinda asked when they were out of hearing range.

"That's Charlie Moffett, my big competition. He won last year and he's been ragging on me and April ever since."

"Then I guess you'll just have to prove who's best."

He grinned at her. "That's exactly what I plan to do."

After a loop around the arena, Daniel returned April to the trailer and tied her up again. "Let's go see if we can find Arnie," he said.

Melinda stroked April's neck and mane. "Will she be all right alone?"

"She'll be fine. Nobody will bother her. It's a cowboy's code of honor thing. Besides, my buddies will look out for her."

As they strolled toward the carnival area, Melinda began to notice the growing number of families with children who were attending. For the past couple of years she'd avoided places where children gathered.

The sight of a happy child being pushed on a swing in a park or held in his mother's arms brought back too many memories. She'd flash back to happy times with Jason. His laughter and his smiles. Then, in a blink, she'd remember that her son was dead. She'd never push him in a swing again. Or hold him in her arms.

The childish screams of excitement all around her were like knives being driven into her ears. She gritted her teeth against what she knew was coming. A full-blown attack.

Panic, like a black cloud of poison gas, expanded in her chest, making each breath she drew painful. The sun narrowed her vision to pinpricks. Sweat formed two rivers, streaming from her temples to her jawline, where they leaped to their death on the dusty ground.

"Melinda?" Daniel's hands closed around her shoulders. He bent to look into her eyes. "Melinda! What's wrong?"

Like swimming in a pool of sun-softened tar, she struggled to return to safe ground. "I'm fine." Her voice seemed distant, coming from a far-off island where she'd banished her memories. To no avail.

"I'm getting you into the shade. I think you're having a heatstroke." He propelled her to the shady side of a red-and-white-striped booth where later in the day home-canned goods would be judged. Jars of peaches and apricots, string beans and beets stood in military rows on a flimsy tabletop. He grabbed a chair and sat her down.

"Put your head between your knees," he ordered.

She did. Slowly the panic, the pain, began to ebb.

"Better?" he asked.

She nodded.

"Stay put. I'm going to get you some water."

She eased her head up, gratified her panic attack had dissipated. She glanced around at the crowd. Apparently no one except Daniel had noticed her odd behavior. Thank goodness. She was embarrassed enough that he'd witnessed the attack.

She hoped he never would again.

A boy of about four broke free from his mother, who was pushing a stroller with two younger children on board. The youngster made a dash for the home-canned goods display.

"Look, Mommy. Our peaches!" He jumped, trying to reach a jar of his mother's peaches.

"Tommy! Come back here," his mother called.

Having failed on his first try, young Tommy made a second attempt. He flung himself upward over the table, knocking over two jars in the process. He hung there a moment, half on the display table, half off, kicking his legs.

The table tilted. Jars began to slide, bumping into their neighbors.

Instinct and adrenaline, the image of the little boy pummeled by heavy jars of fruit and vegetables, drove Melinda to her feet. In two steps, she snatched Tommy from the table. She stepped away just as the table collapsed. Dozens of canning jars came crashing down to the ground. Some broke, spilling their contents. Others rolled into the path of strolling families.

"Tommy!" his mother screamed.

The boy burst into tears.

Daniel came rushing up to Melinda. "What happened?"

"He didn't mean to do it." She tried to soothe the child, but his mother snatched Tommy from her arms.

"I told you to come back, young man! Didn't you hear me?"

Drawn by the excitement, a crowd gathered to see what was going on. An official in charge of judging appeared and sent for help.

Shaking with residual adrenaline, Melinda allowed Daniel to pull her away from the spectacle. He handed her the bottle of water he'd bought, and she drank the cool liquid in gulps.

When she stopped for a breath, he said, "You saved that little boy from getting seriously hurt, didn't you?"

"Yes." A tremor passed through her.

How could she ever forgive herself for not saving her own child?

Chapter Eleven

Daniel pulled Mindy into his arms, holding her close as though she was in need of a rescue as much as the little boy had been. He didn't know what was going on with her. Her eyes wide, her whole body quaking, he'd seen men gored by a bull who looked less shaken than she did.

Whatever was wrong, it was contagious. Daniel's knees threatened to give way. His mouth had dried like a summer drought. His hands kept skimming along her back, more for his own reassurance than hers.

"Can you walk?" he asked.

She gave a quick, jerky nod.

"Good. Let's get out of here." He urged her toward the path that ran behind the booths, away from the crowds, where boxes and other paraphernalia for the booths were stacked. "You going to be okay?"

"Yes."

He barely heard her choked whisper. "Do you want to tell me what happened to you back there?"

This time a jerky shake of her head.

He wanted to help but didn't know how. At least she was steady on her feet now. Her flushed cheeks had returned to normal, her soft skin colored by the sun and heat.

"Maybe if you ate something it would help," he suggested. "Or some iced tea?" She'd downed most of the water he'd given her.

"That'd be fine." Enthusiastic, she wasn't.

Looking around, Daniel got his bearings and headed them toward the chili cook-off area. They hadn't gone far when he realized all he had to do was follow his nose. The rich scent of browned meat, hot chili and spices and simmering tomato sauce permeated the air and made his stomach growl.

In the middle of a long row of blue push-up canopies, they found Arnie and his chili-cooking buddies. Arnie had two giant pots simmering on gas burners. Small cardboard bowls and plastic spoons were set out for folks who wanted to sample his concoctions.

"Hey, bro," Daniel said, reaching down to give Sheila a scratch behind her ears, which kept her tail in happy motion. "I've got a hungry lady here. Think you can fix her up?"

Arnie wheeled his chair around. "Hey, Melinda. It figures my little brother would come lookin' for free food."

She managed an I'm-all-right-now smile. "I've been looking forward to having more of your chili. The last batch was wonderful."

"Watch out for the hot-and-spicy entry," Daniel

warned, pointing to the pot on the left labeled Red Chili.

"But I like spicy food," she protested.

Daniel pointed to a fire extinguisher mounted near the gas burners. "Trust me, that extinguisher isn't there to put out a fire. It's there to save your lips and tonsils if you're foolish enough to take a bite of that rot gut. I swear he's using paint varnish for the base."

She laughed, and relief swept over Daniel. Whatever had set Mindy off, it must've passed.

"Don't believe a word he says." Arnie ladled a bit of the hot-and-spicy version into a bowl. "Those of us with discriminating palates prefer a little spice in our lives." He stuck a spoon in the bowl and handed it to Mindy.

She smiled her thanks, eyed Daniel with what appeared to be a challenge and spooned a bite into her mouth.

"In about three seconds, it'll hit you," Daniel warned. "Arnie, get her a bottle of water, okay?"

Rolling to the back of his booth, Arnie plucked a bottle from the pack of thirty-six and tossed it to Daniel.

"Oh, my." Melinda's eyes widened and began to water. "That's really—"

Daniel unscrewed the cap on the water bottle.

"—hot!"

"I told you so." He handed her the water but she didn't take it.

"Wow! That's what I call chili."

To Daniel's astonishment, she took another bite. Her

mouth and slender throat had to be lined with iron. Her stomach, too.

She turned to Arnie. "That's got to be a winner. How have the judges reacted?"

"They were all taken to the emergency hospital after one bite," Daniel muttered.

Melinda punched him with an elbow to his ribs. Groaning, he staggered backward in mock pain.

"Glad you approve. If I win, I'll go to the World Chili Cook-Off." Arnie shot Daniel a gotcha grin. "Your girl has excellent taste, bro. Except in men, of course, or she wouldn't be hanging around with you."

Daniel sensed a conspiracy in the making. He didn't mind. The two people he cared most about were having fun at his expense. That was fine with him.

He helped himself to a bowl of the milder-flavored chili and listened while the two of them discussed recipes and spices and where they'd eaten the best chili. When a cooling breeze came up, it caught Mindy's straw hat and blew it off. He jogged after it, returning it with a smile. Her blue eyes brightened with appreciation.

Even so, the faint lines of tension at the corners of her eyes still gave away her previous strain, the fear or hysteria she'd experienced earlier. Whatever painful emotion she'd suffered lingered just below the surface.

Daniel wished he knew what was wrong, wished he could help, wished he could make the pain go away.

He glanced at his watch. "Hey, guys, I've gotta get back to the arena and saddle up April and get her ready. You coming?" He directed the question to Mindy.

"Of course," she said.

"I'm coming, too," Arnie said. "Wouldn't want to miss my hotshot brother beating the pants off of Charlie Moffett." He asked a friend to watch after his chili and gear, then wheeled out from behind the table. Sheila took her position at his side.

As Arnie pushed off down the asphalt pathway between the rows of exhibits, Daniel and Melinda had to jog to keep up. Since the accident, Arnie had been compulsive about bodybuilding and exercise, even training for a wheelchair marathon. Daniel couldn't blame him. It was one of the few ways his brother had of controlling his life.

For the afternoon events, the crowd around the arena had swollen considerably. Riders hurried to get their horses ready. Well-trained mounts, sensing the excitement, shied away from their owners, anxious to get started.

Reflecting Daniel's tension, April shook her head and stomped her hoof, first backing away, then bumping him.

"Come on, sweetheart. This is no time to lose your cool," he murmured to the sorrel. "I'm counting on you to do your best." So was Arnie, Daniel recalled. And the bank, for that matter.

The announcer called the cow-cutting event over the loudspeaker and asked for all contestants to gather at the far end of the arena.

Daniel mounted April, took up the reins and settled in the saddle. He wore entry number 1329 pinned on the back of his shirt. "This is it, girl. Don't let me down." He patted April's neck.

"We'll be over by the south gate," Arnie announced. "We'll meet you there."

"Good luck, Daniel." Shading her eyes, Melinda gave him a tentative smile that said she knew what was at stake.

He touched the brim of his hat in a casual salute. "At the end of the day, April will be wearing two blue ribbons. Count on it."

Riding around to the far end of the arena, Daniel tamped down the adrenaline that galloped through his veins. The cow-cutting event required a cool head and precision movements of horse and rider with most of the responsibility resting on the horse's "cow sense" once a cow was separated from the herd.

They joined a dozen other contestants milling around in the marshaling area. Daniel acknowledged the other riders with a nod. When the contestants were all present, the announcer called for the cows and about a dozen were released into the arena and the first rider announced.

"Contestant number 1278, George Pollack, on Sky-hawk."

Daniel watched as the rider entered the ring. He kept his eye on the cows, looking for ones that were too agitated to be easily contained or too determined to stick with the small herd.

George picked an agitated cow that was hard for his horse to control. The judges gave him mediocre points.

Disappointed, George and his horse exited the ring right near the spot where Arnie and Melinda were watching. Daniel smiled. Even from across a rodeo ring, she drew his eye like a thirsty man zeroing in on a pool of cool, spring water.

His turn came in the middle of the pack.

He took his place by the gate. By now the herd had gotten squirrelly, shifting from one corner of the pen to another, leaderless and stirring up a lot of dust that blew across the ring.

"Contestant 1329, Daniel O'Brien, on April." The announcement boomed through the loudspeakers and the gate opened to let Daniel into the ring.

"Here we go," he murmured to April.

The crowd quieted as Daniel trotted toward the herd. The cows swung to the right. April followed. Daniel kept his eye on the cow he'd identified as workable and reined April in that direction. Within seconds, he'd separated the cow from the herd to an audible gasp of approval from the audience.

Daniel released his hold on the reins. April took over on her own, penning the separated cow away from the herd. Every time the cow tried to return to the herd, April blocked her way. First on the right, then on the left, without a single command from Daniel.

The crowd began to applaud. Still April wouldn't let the cow out of her control.

"Thank you, contestant 1329," the announcer said.

Daniel lifted the reins and wheeled April to the center of the ring. He raised his Stetson to the crowd's cheers.

The judges gave him almost perfect scores across the board.

Daniel grinned as he nudged April to a trot toward the exit. "See if you can beat that mark, Charlie."

Dismounting, Daniel joined Melinda and Arnie.

"Well done, Danny boy." Arnie gave his brother a high five.

"Very impressive." Melinda, holding her hat on to keep it from blowing away, patted and stroked April's neck. The smile Daniel received, one that crinkled the corners of her eyes, was meant for him alone.

Six more contestants and the news Daniel had expected came over the loudspeaker. "And the winner of the cow-cutting event is contestant 1329, Daniel O'Brien on April."

To the cheers of the crowd, Daniel rode out to center ring. The head judge pinned a blue ribbon on April's bridle and handed Daniel a check for three thousand dollars.

The tension that he'd been trying to hold at bay eased. His shoulders relaxed. The knot in his stomach loosened. As he rode for the exit, a triumphant shout tried to force its way up his throat. He barely contained it.

He shot a look at Charlie, who had taken third place. The sour look on his face made Daniel silently chortle with glee.

"I'll wipe that grin off your face in the trail event," Charlie promised.

"Not this year." He rode out of the ring and bent down to hand Arnie the check. "One down, one more to go."

During the hour between events, Daniel cooled April down and gave her some water. Melinda brushed the horse and combed out her tail. She hadn't been raised around horses, but during that one summer in Potter Creek, she'd learned to ride and groom them, although not as proficiently as Daniel and Arnie.

There was something soothing about the ripple of muscles under April's skin as she was brushed and the pleasure the horse seemed to receive from the attention.

Closing her eyes, she remembered her mother brushing her hair. She'd felt secure. Loved. Normal.

The blackness of grief threatened to close over her. Would she ever feel that way again?

Daniel hooked his arm over her shoulders. "You okay?"

She looked up and was immediately snared by his dark eyes. A crease of concern drew his brows closer together.

"I'm fine."

"I was worried about you earlier."

"It was nothing. Just the heat," she lied. Only her therapist knew about her panic attacks, her PTSD. She wanted to keep it that way.

Daniel held her gaze for several heartbeats. "I'm a pretty good listener if you ever need to talk."

"I'm fine," she repeated. "Really."

"Okay." He squeezed her shoulders once, then stepped away, leaving her with a feeling of loss. "Gotta saddle up again. They'll be calling the trail event soon."

When Daniel had finished saddling April, he rode to the contestants' assembly area. Arnie and Melinda, with Sheila leading the way, headed to the south gate again.

"Daniel winning this event is important for you two, isn't it?" Melinda asked.

"Winning another first place would make our mortgage payment a lot easier to handle." Despite the uneven ground, he pushed his wheelchair along at a steady pace.

"What if you win the chili cook-off? Do you win a prize, too?"

He glanced up and gave her smile. "Despite your high praise, which I fully appreciate, I'm not going to win. Ralph Parkinson has had that locked up for years. His son-in-law is the head judge."

"That doesn't sound fair."

"Nope, it isn't. Parkinson is also the town mayor, so nobody complains."

"I'd sure complain if someone pulled a stunt like that in a knitting competition."

He laughed and pushed past a family with two young children. Keeping her eyes glued on Arnie's back, Melinda hurried after him. She didn't want to risk another panic attack by paying too much attention to the youngsters. One attack in a day was more than enough.

During the break between activities in the arena, workers had laid out an obstacle course for the trail event.

Spectators who had claimed good viewing spots at the railing gave way for Arnie and his wheelchair, letting him move to the front. Melinda slipped in beside him.

She watched as early contestants urged their horses to cross a narrow bridge, step sideways to go around a low fence and perform various other complicated maneuvers.

Except for a fussy child nearby, the crowd remained silent during the performances. No one wanted to distract the horse and rider. Only when the contestant completed the course did everyone applaud and cheer.

With each contestant, Melinda's stomach tightened and sweat beaded her forehead. She gnawed on her fingernail, something she hadn't done since junior high school. Each horse and rider executed the maneuvers better than the last, and she wondered how Daniel would be able to outperform them.

If she'd known how tight money was on the O'Brien ranch, she never would have let Daniel put her supplies on his credit card. If the bank loaned her the money to expand the shop, and she wasn't optimistic about that, she vowed to pay Daniel back immediately.

The fussy, whiny child nearby grew louder. The little girl, who look to be about three years old and was dressed in a cowgirl skirt and red cowboy hat, squirmed out of her mother's arms.

Daniel and April entered the ring. Daniel looked so comfortable and in charge sitting in the saddle, she concentrated on him. The way he sat so straight in the saddle. How he and the horse effortlessly moved in unison as if their minds were melded together, mastering each new obstacle without a moment's hesitation.

The child's piercing scream broke Melinda's concentration.

She winced and turned in time to see the little girl climb over the bottom rail of the fence and dash into the ring.

"Daddy! Daddy!" the child cried.

"Caroline, come back!" her mother screamed.

Instinct and fear propelled Melinda over the fence. In the girl's impulsive action, she read danger for the child, failure for Daniel.

Melinda's straw hat blew off. She grabbed for it and missed as the hat cartwheeled across the arena, bouncing and skipping like a playful child escaping to romp in a park with his friends.

The little girl veered to the left, her long blond hair bouncing beneath her red cowgirl hat.

Melinda followed. Tears momentarily blurred her vision. She saw Jason running away from her, running toward danger. "Stop!" she cried. *Don't leave me, Jason.*

"Mindy! Come back!" Arnie shouted.

She had to catch up with the little girl. Take her safely back to her mother where she belonged.

Behind her, the crowd groaned. Melinda kept her eyes focused on the child, who seemed to be running in a wide circle.

"Come on, baby," she cried. "I don't want you to get hurt." Breathless, her muscles burning, she pursued the youngster. Just a few more steps...

The little girl climbed through the fence. Her mother scooped her up into her arms.

Melinda slammed into the same fence. She gasped for air. The child was safe.

"Contestant 1329 is disqualified. Exceeded the time limit" blared over the loudspeaker.

A loud groan rose from the crowd.

Melinda whirled. How could they—

Daniel galloped toward her. Even at a distance, she could see the concern in his expression. The worry. Eyebrows lowered. Jaw set.

Panic rose in her chest. Helplessly, she looked toward Arnie.

He shook his head. "Your hat. It spooked April when it blew past them. She balked at the bridge. He had to try again."

Her hands flew to her face. Bile rose in her throat. Her heart missed a beat, then thundered in her ears.

No. Oh, no. What had she done?

Chapter Twelve

Desperate to get to Mindy, Daniel spurred April toward her at a gallop. He reined the mare to a halt only feet from Mindy and leapt to the ground.

"I'm so sorry." Guilt and misery were written in her furrowed brow and sorrowful eyes, the constriction of her voice. "I'm so very sorry."

He cupped her chin and forced her gaze up to meet his. "What were you doing? Why did you run out into the arena?" When he'd seen her hat blowing across the arena, he'd lost his concentration and turned to see what was happening. That instant of inattention had cost him and April the event. And the prize money. He had only himself to blame.

"The child. The little girl."

He shook his head. "What are you talking about?"

Frantically, she looked around at the crowd of on-lookers pressed against the arena fence gawking at them. "She's about three. She had on a little red cowgirl hat. She ran out—" Her words broke on a sob.

His brain sluggish, he tried to process what she was telling him. "You tried to chase after a little girl to rescue her?"

She nodded. "I'm so sorry. I wasn't thinking."

No, she hadn't been *thinking,* he realized. She'd been *reacting,* just as she had earlier in the day with the little boy who'd knocked over the canning jars. But why? he wanted to know. Why such a powerful instinct to protect little kids?

She'd told him she didn't have any children.

"Come on. Let's get you out of here." He grabbed April's reins and ushered Mindy toward the exit. The next contestant was ready to go. They had to clear the ring.

Arnie met them outside the gate. "Tough luck, bro."

"Yeah, I know." He handed the reins to his brother. "Look, I've got to get her away from here. I'm going to take her home. Can you get some of the guys to cool April down, hook the trailer up to your van?"

"Sure, I can do that." He glanced at Mindy. "My brother will take good care of you. He's gotten pretty good at the job."

She barely acknowledged Arnie's comment. Instead she appeared to be in shock, her face pale, her eyes glassy.

Dwayne, one of the teenagers from church, came running over to him. He had Mindy's hat in his hand.

"Is Ms. Spencer okay?" Dwayne handed Daniel the hat.

"She'll be fine, thanks."

Daniel took Mindy by the hand, her fingers icy cold, and the crowd opened a path for them as he led her away from the arena to his truck. He boosted her into the cab and unhooked the horse trailer. From the ice chest in the back of the truck he got a couple bottles of water and climbed behind the steering wheel.

"I'll pay you back," she said, her voice dull and lifeless. "For the loan and for the prize money you lost because of me. I don't know how, but I will. I promise."

He handed her the water. "Don't worry about the money, Goldilocks. Let's worry about you first." Starting the truck, he eased out into a parade of pedestrians walking to and from the arena.

"I never should have come back here."

His stomach clenched. "Aunt Martha needed you." So had he, Daniel realized in a flash of self-awareness. When had that happened? Ten years ago? Or the day he'd discovered her trying to get into Aunt Martha's knitting shop? The day he'd realized he never should have let her leave the first time.

If DeeDee Pickens were still around, he swore he'd… He let the thought slide. He'd learned that anger didn't fix a thing. It wasn't his job to judge the woman. He'd let God be in charge.

It seemed like forever before he made his way out of the fairgrounds and onto the highway heading home.

Mindy hadn't said a word. She sat quietly holding on to the bottle of water with both hands as if it was a saddle horn and she was afraid she was going to get bucked off the horse. Maybe that's how she felt on the inside, barely holding on to her emotions.

What had happened to her back in Pittsburgh that had made her so on edge around kids one minute and rushing to protect them the next?

He cruised past the exit to Potter Creek.

"Hey." She looked back over her shoulder. "You missed the exit."

"Nope. I'm taking you to the ranch."

Her head snapped around. "But Martha—"

"She'll be fine. She's probably not expecting you back for hours yet. You and I need to talk."

Her hard stare raised the hackles on the back of his neck.

"We don't have anything to talk about," she said. "I've apologized. I've promised I'll get the money as soon as I can. What else do you want?"

As easy as can be, he rested his hand on hers, the hand that held the water bottle in a death grip. "I care about you, Melinda. I want to know what's going on with you, and I want to fix it, if I can."

He heard a catch in her throat and a sob. She pushed his hand away. "You can't fix it."

Putting his hand back on the steering wheel, he said, "That's not going to stop me from trying."

When he drove beneath the arched entrance to O'Brien Ranch, she straightened in the seat, her attention caught as they passed the horse pasture.

"You've made some changes."

"Here and there," he conceded, unable to keep the pride from his voice. He and his brother had worked their tails off to make the ranch a profitable enterprise. They hadn't quite made it yet, but they would. Assuming they could keep the bankers at bay.

He parked near the back porch.

"There wasn't any need to bring me here," she said. "I'm fine now."

"I'll be the judge of that, Goldilocks."

He walked around to the passenger side and opened the door for her. She sat unmoving, staring out the windshield.

"You can get out and walk inside under your own power. Or I can carry you inside. Your choice."

Hat in hand, she hesitated a moment before swinging her legs around and hopping down to the ground. "I hope you know kidnapping's illegal."

His lips twitched with the threat of a smile. She sounded almost like herself now, but he wasn't going to lay off until he found out what was going on beneath those bouncy curls of hers.

He walked her through the kitchen and into the living room, seeing for the first time how run-down the furniture had become and how the clutter of magazines had grown, overrunning every horizontal surface. The only new item in the room for the past ten years was a fifty-inch flat-screen TV.

"Can I get you something to eat or drink?" he asked.

"No, thank you." Brittle words that matched her expression. She was still about to crack.

He cleared magazines and newspapers off the couch. "Take a seat, Mindy."

"So you can interrogate me?"

"So we can talk."

She tossed her hat on the end table and sat at the far end of the couch. Folding her legs beneath her, she grabbed both of her elbows and pulled her arms against her chest like a shield. She looked as though she had a broomstick for a spine. She didn't meet his gaze.

Sitting down on the coffee table right in front of her, Daniel leaned forward, resting his arms on his thighs. "So tell me what happened when you went back home to Pittsburgh."

Her gaze slid toward him. "I finished my senior year and got a job in a knitting shop." She shrugged as though that was the end of her story.

"Where did you meet your husband?"

Her forehead puckered. "I knew him from school. Joe was a year ahead of me."

Daniel quashed a spark of jealousy. This was not the time. "Nice guy?"

"Yes."

"What did he do for a living?"

"What does that have to do with anything?" She freed her elbows to clasp her hands together. "His father owned a transportation company. Long-haul big rigs."

"So Joe was gone a lot?"

"Not really. Not at first. He mostly worked in the office doing dispatch." She glanced away, toward the kitchen, toward escape.

Daniel latched on to the "not at first" comment. "But after a while, he started to stay away more? Drive a truck for long hauls?"

"No, not his father's trucks. He—" Her voice cracked. "He signed up with a civilian contractor to drive trucks in Afghanistan."

Daniel reared back like he'd been punched in the gut. "Why'd he do that?"

"Because…" Tears sheened her eyes. "We needed the money."

Sure, he knew the truckers over there made big bucks, but there had to have been another choice. One that wasn't so potentially fatal. "Is that where he died?"

Nodding, she covered her mouth with the fingers of her right hand. A tear slipped down her cheek. "I told him he could go. I practically forced him to go, drove him to it. The medical bills were so huge and we couldn't—"

"You were sick?"

"No, not me." Her breath shuddered. More tears followed the first one until there was a steady trail leaking from her eyes.

Daniel wasn't sure she was aware she was crying. He hated himself for making her relive her pain and grief. He wanted to back off. Not ask any more questions. But he was confused and couldn't let it go.

"If you weren't sick, who was?"

"Jason." She gulped, her throat working furiously. "Our son."

"*Your son?* I thought you said—"

"He died. They both died. It was my fault. Both of them. I tried so hard to keep Jason alive. I prayed and prayed. I wouldn't give up hope. I couldn't." Her words ran together like stampeding horses. Her voice rose, shrill and painful. "I'd already lost Joe. I'd driven him away. It was my fault he died. I didn't want to lose my baby, too. And then the doctors said—" Her eyes were wide. She wiped her mouth with the back of her hand but ignored her tears. "I let them take him off the respirator. I told them it was okay. I gave permission. I let them kill my baby boy."

Stunned, speechless, Daniel's head spun.

Standing, he tried to calm his thoughts. He paced across the room, a feeling of helplessness pressed on his chest making breathing almost impossible. She'd lost her husband. Her son. He couldn't imagine the pain she'd been through. The weight of guilt that over-whelmed her.

"Your son. Jason. He was in a coma?"

She nodded. "They'd tried to shrink the tumor in his brain. They'd tried everything. I wanted them to keep trying, but the doctors said there was no point."

"How did he…" He barely knew what questions to ask. Or if he should ask any question. "When did you first realize there was something wrong?"

She looked up at Daniel, her eyes glistening with tears she hadn't yet shed. "He was such a beautiful little boy. Blond and rambunctious. All boy. He loved airplanes and trucks like his daddy drove. And cars. He'd play with his little cars and make them sound like race cars." Her hand covered her mouth again in an effort to hold back another sob.

In two steps, Daniel was kneeling in front of her, taking her hands in his. "You don't have to tell me, Goldilocks. It's okay."

"No, it's not. I need to tell someone. It hurts so much."

Her pain became his and twisted through his gut like a double-edged knife. He knew about feeling guilt but not the pain of loss.

"He was about two. He had a seizure. The doctors said it was nothing. A high fever. But it wasn't nothing. Soon after that he started to stumble. He'd always been so quick on his feet. He could outrun every other child at his day care, except he started to fall down for no reason at all. He'd just fall over."

Bringing her hands to his lips, he kissed them. "It's okay, Mindy. It's okay."

"No, it wasn't okay. Everything got worse. He had headaches and backaches. He cried incessantly. Joe hated that, but Jason couldn't help it. He was just a little baby. He forgot how to talk, how to tell Mommy what was wrong. He'd look at me with his big blue eyes and I couldn't help him."

"Oh, baby, I'm so sorry." He shifted from kneeling to sitting on the couch beside her, holding her. He'd never known anyone who'd gone through so much. Yet she'd had the courage to move to Montana. To start over. He wasn't sure if he'd endured what she had that he could have been half as brave.

"We took Jason to doctor after doctor. Our insurance started refusing our claims. Finally…" Her whole body shuddered. "An MRI showed Jason had a tumor. An inoperable brain tumor."

Wincing, Daniel held her even closer.

She leaned her head against his shoulder. Her tears

dampened his shirt. He stroked her hair trying to soothe her. "How long...?"

She shuddered again as she drew another breath. "He was five when he died. My baby."

She felt vulnerable in his arms, fragile and so incredibly courageous. How had she endured the grief? Three years of struggle to try to save her son only to lose him in the end. She'd waged an epic battle and lost.

Little wonder she'd reacted so strongly to some other child she saw as being in danger. In her mind, she must have believed that if she could rescue another child, she'd somehow make up for losing her son.

Because he didn't know what to say or do, he started to rock her back and forth. Her body was lax now; the fight had gone out of her. So he held her and rocked her and prayed the Lord would give him guidance.

But as the light outside faded into twilight, no answer came to him.

The sound of the back door slamming shut startled Daniel.

"Arnie's home," he whispered.

She lifted her head, then jerked back from him. "I don't want Arnie to see me this way." She scrubbed her eyes with the heels of her hands.

"Don't worry about it. He'll just think I did something to hurt your feelings."

Scrambling off the couch, she straightened her blouse and ran her fingers through her hair, keeping her back to the kitchen. "I'd like to go back to Aunt Martha's now."

"Sure, I—"

Arnie wheeled into the living room with Sheila right behind him. "Oh-oh. Did I interrupt something?"

His tone suggested Daniel and Mindy had been doing something other than talking. Daniel didn't try to dissuade his brother.

"I was about to take Mindy home," Daniel said.

"She could stay for supper. I've got leftover chili."

Her head down, her long hair pulled forward to block her face, Mindy shook her head. She eased past Arnie without looking at him and headed toward the back door.

Arnie gave Daniel a hard stare. "What's up?"

"I'll tell you later."

"April's still in the trailer," Arnie reminded him.

"I'll get her. Thanks."

By the time Daniel had put April out to pasture and climbed into the truck, Mindy had her stoic face on. She sat primly, her hands folded in her lap, her gaze straight ahead.

Wheeling the truck around, Daniel headed down the drive to the road.

"I know you've been through a lot, Mindy. I can't imagine how hard losing your husband and your son must've been on you. But none of it was your fault."

"I practically drove Joe away. I ignored him month after month. When the medical bills got so big, he asked me about Afghanistan. I told him to go."

"You didn't kill him. A terrorist did. You didn't cause your son's death, either."

"No, I gave permission for the doctors to do that for me."

He reached the state highway that bordered the ranch and stopped the truck. "The kind of guilt you're carrying isn't good for you, Mindy. It'll eat you up and leave you completely empty inside. Whatever you think you did, whatever you're feeling guilty about, you have to forgive yourself."

Her head snapped around. "How can I forgive myself when I don't deserve God's forgiveness?"

Puffing out his lips, he blew out a sigh. He knew exactly what a massive struggle it was to forgive oneself and to accept the Lord's forgiveness.

"He forgave me, Mindy. But I had to forgive myself first."

Chapter Thirteen

Sunday morning, in an effort to stay home from church, Melinda pleaded a headache and fatigue, both of which were true. But her real reason to skip church was to avoid facing Daniel again so soon.

"I'm sorry you're not feeling well, dear," Aunt Martha said. "We'll stay home today and watch Reverend Tolliver on television. His sermons are quite powerful and the choir sings praise hymns like none other."

So Melinda took two aspirins, put on a load of wash and sat with Aunt Martha listening to Reverent Tolliver praise the Lord and insist that God was a forgiving God. Melinda knew that wasn't true.

Daniel was wrong, too. There was nothing she could do to gain God's forgiveness. Why would He forgive her? She'd sent Joe to his death. She'd held Jason in her arms and let him die.

Now, added to her sins, she'd cost Daniel the three thousand dollars of prize money he should have won for the trail event.

Was there no end to her transgressions?

* * *

After lunch, she drove to Manhattan to do a week's worth of grocery shopping. When she returned, Daniel's truck was parked in front of Aunt Martha's house.

She groaned and her shoulders slumped. The man simply didn't know how to quit.

Tempted to keep driving and not come back until he'd gone away, she pictured herself going all the way to Pittsburgh. But there was nothing left for her there. Only memories that sucked at her soul, memories she carried with her every minute of every day.

Besides, the chicken she'd bought to roast for dinner would spoil and the chocolate ice cream would melt.

With a sigh, she pulled Aunt Martha's old Buick into the driveway. She popped the trunk, grabbed two grocery sacks and walked up the steps.

Daniel pushed open the screen door for her. He'd evidently changed into jeans and a work shirt since the morning church service. At least he hadn't come calling dressed in his Sunday finery.

She moved past him, unable to look him in the eye.

"I brought your hat back. You left it at the house yesterday."

"Thank you."

In the kitchen, she put the groceries on the counter. Aunt Martha was sitting at the table as were two glasses of iced tea.

"Daniel stopped by to bring your hat back. Isn't he a sweet young man." Aunt Martha's speech had improved markedly since she'd come home from the rehab facility.

She barely slurred her words now. Her right hand still wasn't as strong as it should be, however. "I told him you'd be home soon."

Unsettled, Melinda turned to go back to the car for more groceries and practically slammed into the middle of Daniel's chest. Or rather the middle of the three bags of groceries he was carrying in his muscular arms.

"I'll get the rest of the groceries," she said.

"No, I'll get 'em. You can put the groceries away." His lips quirked into a very annoying smile. "It's called teamwork."

Why would he want her to play on his team? She'd already cost him a bundle of money.

"Is everything all right, dear?" Aunt Martha asked. "You seem a little tense. Is your headache still bothering you?"

"Just a little, but I'm fine, Aunt Martha." The thunder in her head was louder than a summer storm and all due to Daniel's unexpected presence.

She pulled the items out of the grocery sacks that needed to be refrigerated.

Daniel returned with two more bags of groceries. "Hey, I spotted some ice cream. You going on a chocolate bender?" He plucked the gallon of double-dark chocolate from the bag and held it up for her inspection.

"It's for purely medicinal purposes." She snatched the container from him and shoved it into the freezer.

"When you're done putting everything away, dear, why don't you fix yourself and Daniel a bowl of ice cream? You could sit on the back porch and chat while I take a little nap."

Melinda shot her aunt a quelling look. Was she trying to play matchmaker?

"Sounds good to me," Daniel said as he unloaded one of the sacks.

"Have a nice snack, then." Aunt Martha stood and kerthump-thumped slowly out of the kitchen with her walker.

Didn't Daniel realize she'd stayed away from church because she couldn't face him?

She hated that she'd cried in front of him. Bawled like a baby and soaked his nice Western shirt in the process. She'd felt so vulnerable. Weak.

Which was exactly what she hadn't wanted to do after acting so stupidly at the festival.

PTSD had apparently turned her into a raving lunatic, trying to rescue every kid who was in any kind of trouble. Which was ridiculous. She couldn't even rescue herself. *You have to forgive yourself.* Daniel's words had rattled around in her head all night. They were still in there taunting her now. How would that ever be possible?

She'd have to forget her husband. Forget Jason. Forget what she'd done. She'd never do that.

With the groceries put away, Daniel retrieved the ice cream from the freezer and found the bowls in the cupboard. "How much do you want?"

The need for chocolate, the rich flavor, flooded her mouth. "The whole gallon."

His chuckle sent gooseflesh zipping down her spine.

"I'll start you off with a big bowlful and then you can have more if you want it."

She sighed and took the dish he'd handed her and got two spoons from the drawer.

Since she'd arrived in Potter Creek, she'd washed off the wicker slider on the back porch. A few evenings she and her aunt had sat there watching the sky color and fade into darkness. Now she wished she'd brought out another chair so she wouldn't have to sit so close to Daniel. While their thighs weren't actually touching, she could feel his heat and catch the scent of his spicy aftershave.

With only a songbird and an occasional passing car on Main Street breaking the silence of a Sunday afternoon, Melinda let the cold ice cream and rich chocolate flavor soothe her.

"Did your aunt tell you how Arnie was injured?" Daniel asked.

Her hand hovered over the ice cream, poised to scoop up another bite. "She said there'd been an accident."

"The story's a little more complicated than that." He pushed off with his booted foot to start the glider swinging. "I was driving and we were in my old battered truck. The same one I had when you were here before."

An old, green Chevy pickup with a dented fender and lopsided bumper, she remembered, an edgy feeling of discomfort pricking the back of her neck.

"I'd taken a shortcut to Harrison and was showing off. I got that bucket of bolts up close to seventy miles an hour on that narrow dirt road. Rocks were flying up, hitting the undercarriage, and we were bouncing around on the ruts like we were on board a bucking bronco. Arnie asked me to slow down. I didn't. I actually laughed at him and pushed the accelerator down all the way."

Melinda thought she knew the rest of the story and didn't want to hear the ending.

"I went roaring into a curve and hit a big pothole. The impact yanked the steering wheel out of my hands. We went off the road over an embankment. I remember seeing this big ol' boulder coming right at me." He stared into the distance for a moment, then put the dish down on the porch. "When I came to, Arnie was crumpled on the ground like a rag doll about fifteen feet from the truck." His voice quavered. "I thought I'd killed him."

Melinda held her breath. He didn't have to say he'd felt guilty. She could hear the guilt in his voice, see the guilt in the way he lowered his head and clenched his hands together, smell the guilt on the air like the stench of rotten peaches.

She knew that feeling well. The putrefaction that touched every part of her life.

"But he didn't die," she said softly.

"Came close, though. He had a broken back, broken hip and a serious concussion. The doctors were afraid his brain would swell and they had to drill holes in his head to ease the pressure."

She shuddered and put her dish down, too. "Were you hurt?"

"I got off easy. A couple of cracked ribs and my ankle was busted. It still acts up on rainy days."

Given the circumstances, Melinda imagined he hadn't thought his survival was *easy*. If he was anything like her, despite their years of sibling bickering, he would have gladly changed places with Arnie.

Just as she would have given her life for Jason.

Daniel stood and walked to the porch railing, looking out at the overgrown backyard. "Arnie went through months of rehab. He'll never walk again but he's stronger now than he ever was. Stronger than me."

"Seeing your brother like that must have been hard on you."

"Oh, yeah. I went a little crazy, I think." He half turned toward her and rested his hip on the railing. "The thing is, Arnie never blamed me. He kept saying it was an accident. Not my fault. Stuff happens. I knew different. I couldn't stop blaming myself. My guilt took over my whole life. I could hardly eat or drink. I had nightmares, relived that crash a thousand times."

The muscles in her throat tightened. He'd had PTSD. Those flashbacks were part of the syndrome. The painful memories that wouldn't go away.

She had to speak past the constriction in her throat. "Do the flashbacks ever stop?"

"They do, Mindy. But first I had to forgive myself." He sat down next to her again and rested his arm on the back of the slider. "You may remember I wasn't much of a churchgoer ten years ago."

Her lips twitched ever so slightly. The baddest bad

boy of Potter Creek had had no time for the Lord. He preferred to play hard and fast.

"Arnie finally insisted I go talk with Reverend Redmond. It took the pastor, Arthur, a while to get through my thick skull, but I got it eventually. He said that not forgiving myself for what I'd done, however awful it was, was a form of pride. Egotism. Like *I'm* more important than what God wants me to be."

Staring into Daniel's eyes, seeing his intensity, his belief, Melinda struggled to understand and accept what he was saying. "Even if I could forgive myself for what happened to Joe and my son, God never would."

"You're wrong, Goldilocks. God does not choose to forgive one person and not the other. If you believe in Jesus Christ, He forgives you. It's a done deal as soon as you forgive yourself and ask Him."

Her headache started again and she rubbed her temple with her fingertips. "It can't be that easy."

"It is, Mindy. I promise." He brushed a light kiss to her forehead as if to take away her pain. "Talk with Pastor Redmond. You don't have to torture yourself any longer. He'll tell you I'm right."

Chapter Fourteen

After talking with Melinda, Daniel drove back to the ranch. He didn't know if he'd gotten through to her about the guilt business. It had sure taken him a while to catch on.

There were still days—those days when he had to watch Arnie struggle to accomplish a task that used to be easy for him—that the guilt smacked him in the chest again.

But as the pastor said, you cannot change what has happened.

Daniel found he could give back some of what he'd taken away from Arnie by being the kind of brother he should've been all along.

He found Arnie in the barn working on an old saddle, a cleaning rag in his hand.

Sheila trotted over to greet Daniel. He knelt to give her a good scratch around her ears and neck. "You been fetching and carrying for your boss, girl?"

"I'm going to teach her to climb a ladder so she can

retrieve stuff I can't reach." A can of saddle soap sat on the workbench beside Arnie.

"You want me to get something for you?"

"Naw, I'm good." He smeared a gob of soap on the seat of the saddle and rubbed it in. "How's Melinda?"

Idly, Daniel picked up an old cotton lead rope that had frayed. He tugged on the two ends. Last night he'd told Arnie what went on in Pittsburgh and why she'd been crying. "She feels a lot of guilt about what happened to her husband and son, none of which was her fault."

"Doesn't change the guilt, though, does it?"

"Doing that takes a lot of work." He tugged on the rope again and it split, hanging together by only a few threads. Daniel guessed that was what was happening to Mindy. She was hanging on by a thread. "I told her to talk to the pastor."

"Good."

Sheila turned toward the barn door a moment before a pickup truck drove up and stopped.

"We got company," Daniel said, tossing the frayed rope into a nearby trash barrel. He strolled out to see who had arrived.

Going from the dimly lit barn into the bright sun made him squint. He eyed the driver of the pickup as he climbed out and a spurt of anger whipped through his chest.

Charlie Moffett? Was he stopping by to rag on Daniel about being disqualified in the trail event?

Daniel stuffed his hands in his front pockets and held his ground. "If you're here to gloat, you can get back in your truck and head on home. You've got plenty to write on your Facebook page without coming around here."

Charlie kept on coming, slow and easy. A big man, he stood over six-five and weighed in at more than two hundred pounds. There'd been a time when he was the county arm-wrestling champ, and his biceps still looked as if he could hold his own against any challenger.

"I'm not here to gloat," he said. "In fact, I'm here to apologize."

Daniel blinked. "For what? Losing to me in the cow-cutting event? You want a rematch or something?"

"Nope. My wife gave me the whole story about how that hat spooked your horse and why. My daughter Caroline had gone running out into the ring. A woman chased her trying to save her, to get her to come back. It was her hat that blew off."

"Yeah, I know that." Mindy did stuff like that. Rescue kids. Daniel hadn't known it was Charlie's kid Mindy was trying to rescue, though. That gave the incident a strange twist.

"Up till the hat business, you and your horse were right on. You should've won, not me."

Daniel wasn't about to argue with him. "Thanks. I appreciate the thought."

"I brought you the check for the prize money." He pulled a piece of paper out of his shirt pocket. "This rightfully belongs to you. Maybe you can thank that quick-thinking gal who went after Caroline for us. Our little girl might've been hurt out there. My wife and I are grateful for what that gal did."

His jaw coming unhinged, his eyes wide, Daniel tried to think of a response. He'd have to recalibrate his judgment of Charlie. He'd tell Mindy what Charlie had said. That ought to lift some of the guilt she was carrying on those slender shoulders of hers.

"You earned that money fair and square," Daniel said. "I lost my concentration and so did April. A straw hat blowing around isn't an excuse for losing and it sure wasn't your fault."

"Take it, Danny." Charlie stepped closer, his hand outstretched, the check held between his big, meaty fingers. "Take it because I've got a business proposition for you."

Not entirely sure he should trust Charlie, Daniel took the check, read the amount and stuffed it in his shirt pocket. With his winnings in the cow-cutting event plus what he and Arnie had saved up from the sale of their cattle and breeding activities, and now this check, the mortgage payment due on the ranch was as good as done.

"So what's your proposition?"

First thing Monday morning, a woman came into Knitting and Notions looking for some yarn.

Delighted to have a customer so early in the day, Melinda greeted her with a friendly smile. "Good morning. Can I help you with something?"

"I was talking to Jayne Audis yesterday at church and telling her how I needed a birthday present for my mother." The woman was attractively dressed and probably in her fifties with streaks of gray in her dark brown hair. "Jayne reminded me how much I used to enjoy knitting and suggested I come by the shop. My mother is hard to buy for. She has everything she needs and doesn't want her house filled up with knickknacks. But she's always enjoyed gifts that I've knitted for her."

"It's the personal touch that's so meaningful." Melinda would be sure to thank Jayne for the referral. "Do you have something special in mind?"

"Actually, I do. I thought she might like a felted purse, but I don't have any patterns for one."

"Well, then, let's take a look and see what we can find."

Melinda led her to the pattern books and pulled out a couple she knew contained patterns for purses. The woman thumbed through the pages, rejecting some patterns and studying others more closely.

"You know, I think my mother would like this diagonal ripple effect with a variegated blue on a black background. It would go with almost every outfit she owns. It would be good for the fall, too."

"That sounds perfect. Let's see if I have the yarn the pattern calls for in the colors you want."

Within minutes of opening the shop, Melinda rang up the sale of two skeins of yarn and some new needles. An excellent beginning for the week.

When the wind chimes over the shop door sounded a few minutes later and Daniel stepped inside, Melinda's stomach tightened. The muscles under her left eye started to twitch again. She hadn't yet absorbed what he'd told her yesterday afternoon and wasn't ready to start that conversation all over again.

"Hey, Goldilocks. I've got good news for you."

She pulled her inventory book out from under the counter. "Daniel, we did a lot of talking yesterday. I'm not up to round two just yet."

"Then I'll make this short." He pulled something out of his shirt pocket. "I'm on my way to the bank to deposit the prize money for the trail event."

"You mean cow-cutting." She'd cost him the win in the trail competition.

"Nope." He pulled out a second check and put it on the counter beside the first. Both of them written for three thousand dollars.

She gaped at the checks, then lifted her head. "What'd you do? Waylay Charlie Moffett in the dark of night and steal his check?"

"Now, I'm hurt you think I'd do a thing like that." He put his hand over his heart in mock pain. "Charlie came by the ranch yesterday and gave me the check. Said I would've won the event except for some brave young woman who ran out into the arena to rescue *his* little girl."

"Caroline is Charlie's daughter?"

"Yep. He and his wife are very grateful for your fast thinking and trying to protect Caroline." He scooped up both checks and put them back in his pocket. "So, sweet Goldilocks…" he ran his finger down her nose and tapped it right on the tip "…you no longer have any reason to feel guilty about me not winning the prize money. Plus, Charlie and I are going into business together."

Blinking in reaction to both the touch of his fingertip

and the news about his partnership with his longtime nemesis, Melinda sat down on the stool behind the counter.

"What kind of business?"

"Charlie was smart enough to realize my April and his horse Arapaho are the two best cutting and trail-riding horses in central Montana. The rest of our herds are top-quality quarter horses, too. We're going to start a joint breeding effort that could double the price of the foals we produce."

The excitement in Daniel's eyes nearly blinded her. The dark irises dilated and glowed with intensity, reflecting the overhead lights in the shop.

"That is good news. I'm happy for you. And Charlie."

"So now making the mortgage payment is a snap and the future is looking bright. It's all because you tried to rescue a little girl before she could get hurt."

"That's not really… You know why I—"

He reached across the counter, hooked his hand around the back of her head and pulled her closer for a kiss.

A kiss that took her back ten years, to quiet times by a river that tumbled over a rocky bottom, singing a special love song meant only for her and Daniel.

Chapter Fifteen

After enjoying a relatively busy Monday at the shop, Tuesday was a flop. Fortunately, the church youth group was due in the afternoon. Melinda looked forward to seeing the young people.

She wasn't quite so sure about seeing Daniel.

The kiss they'd shared had slipped into her dreams last night and had niggled at her all day. She shouldn't be thinking about Daniel O'Brien. Not about his kiss. Not about his hand drawing her to him.

When Ivy Nelson from the diner showed up early for class, Melinda was actually relieved. At least the young woman would keep her mind off Daniel's disturbing kiss and her own reaction to it.

"I finished my square for the lap robe," Ivy announced, producing the finished product from her knitting bag and placing the navy blue square on the counter.

"That's wonderful. You're the first one to finish." Melinda noted Ivy's stitches were very even without a single error in the alternating rows of knit and purl. For a young woman with no real interest in knitting, she'd done a fine job for her first effort.

"Yeah, well, I worked on it some when we weren't busy at the diner." She glanced around the shop. "Frankly, that was really boring to make."

Melinda suspected Ivy's general attitude was one of boredom. "Maybe you'd like to try something a little more challenging?"

Although no longer an adolescent, Ivy's world-weary shrug made her look like a sixteen-year-old.

"You were wearing a sweater-vest the other day at the diner that looked okay."

Melinda's brows edged upward. "Thank you. That's something I made for myself. Do you think you'd like to try knitting one of those?"

"Maybe. It can't be too hard, can it?"

"Not at all. You just have to be careful to follow the pattern and use the right gauge yarn."

"I thought maybe I could change it a little." She unfolded a sheet of drawing paper. "See, I wanted the ribbing to be a little wider and the vest to be more fitted through the middle."

Studying the pencil drawing, Melinda was struck with how detailed and artistic Ivy's vision of the vest looked. She'd used colored pencils that made the pattern stand out, almost as though the sweater was in motion like waves on an ocean. She'd created a significant design improvement on the basic pattern, too. "You drew this?" she asked.

"Yeah. It's just a sketch. No big deal."

"It may be no big deal to you, but I'm impressed." Thinking, she tilted her head to the side to study Ivy more carefully. Her makeup was always applied with a light hand, the outfits she wore had a certain youthful flare to them and the colors enhanced her features. "By any chance, did you paint that watercolor I noticed on the wall of the diner? The one of the Rockies with the woman standing alone in the valley?"

"A long time ago."

"You captured a lot of emotion in that painting. You're a very talented artist, Ivy."

A blush colored her cheeks. "My dad doesn't think so."

Shame on her father for not valuing his daughter's God-given aptitude. "Have you taken art classes or studied art anywhere?"

Ivy snorted. "I took one class in high school. I wanted to go to college and major in art, but my dad said that would be a waste of my time and his money. I had to take typing instead."

Melinda strongly disagreed. "You know what? I think what you've drawn here could be a pattern that you could sell to knitting magazines. I can help you work out the stitches and teach you the knitting terms and abbreviations. But the bottom line is, you have talent, young lady."

Her eyes widened. "You think so?"

"Absolutely."

"And I could make money selling patterns?"

"Not enough to make you rich, but a little extra income anyway."

"Enough to pay for art classes at the community college?"

"Oh, yes, I would think so. You'd have to produce new patterns consistently so the publishers would trust your abilities."

Her smile started slowly, as if she wasn't sure Melinda was telling her the truth, and then widened until it lit her eyes. "Wow!"

Impulsively, Melinda hugged Ivy. Obviously, she'd misjudged the young woman. Her actions, her almost-desperate need for attention, was a product of her loneliness and a father who didn't understand her dreams. Ivy Nelson was the young woman standing alone in the painting surrounded by gigantic, cold mountains with no means of escape. At its heart, the painting was Ivy's self-portrait.

Melinda may have just thrown Ivy a lifeline. She hoped so.

It wasn't long before Grace Staples came into the shop with her completed baby cap for her soon-to-be-born nephew. She eyed Ivy with suspicion before handing the cap to Melinda.

"Oh, that's adorable," Melinda said. "You did such a nice job. Your sister will love it."

"I hope so." Grace flushed with pride.

"You finished this so quickly, you still have time to make a little matching sweater for him. That'd be very cute."

"Oh, I thought about it, but now I don't know…"

"It's up to you," Melinda said. "Why don't you

browse through the pattern books, see if anything inspires you."

Grace's gaze fell on the sketch of the sweater vest. "This is awesome. Maybe I should make something like this for myself."

"It's Ivy's design," Melinda told her. "Personally, I'm envious. I wish I could design something that original."

Grace's head snapped up and she stared at Ivy as though the young woman had grown a second head. "You really did this?"

"Sure. It's no biggie," she declared for a second time that afternoon. But this time there was a ton of self-respect in her voice.

The two girls started talking about the vest and how Ivy had come up with a new design. Smiling to herself, Melinda greeted the other members of the class as they arrived.

Soon all the girls were gathered around Ivy, filled with questions and new respect. The boys, of course, were less impressed with her artistic prowess.

Even though her back was to the door, Melinda knew the moment Daniel arrived with his brother. Before any of the kids noticed Daniel, she felt his gaze skim over her like a warm caress. Sensed how he filled the shop with his elemental masculinity.

Turning, his black eyes snared her with questions she didn't dare answer. Questions about second chances.

Her mouth as dry as a summer wind, she said, "Hey, Arnie. Daniel. How's your knitting going?"

"Slowly," Arnie said. "But I'm getting there."

"I was pretty busy over the weekend." Daniel winked at her and his smile spoke volumes about the kiss they had shared. "Had other things on my mind."

So had Melinda.

"Well…" She cleared her throat and turned away from Daniel's penetrating gaze. "Let's get started, shall we?"

For the next hour, Melinda found herself retrieving dropped stitches and ripping out rows of knitting that had to be redone. No one seemed to mind, though. In fact, most of the youngsters were doing a good job with their respective afghan squares. Within another week, they should have a completed project to send off to a military hospital.

About the time the class was breaking up, the mail carrier brought in a handful of letters and advertising flyers. He nodded to her and placed the mail on the counter.

"Everyone," she said to the class. "Let's all see if you can finish up your square this week. Then I'll show you how to stitch it all together into our afghan."

Ivy raised her hand. "Ms. Spencer, you said when we send off the afghan to a soldier, we can put a note inside with it."

"Yes, that's true."

"Would it be all right if I made up a big card that we could all write a note on and sign?"

Melinda looked around at the class. No one seemed to have an objection. "I think that's an excellent idea, Ivy. Thank you for suggesting it."

The young woman smiled shyly, eyeing the others to see if they approved.

"All right, then," Melinda said. "I'll see you all again on Thursday. And no dropped stitches this week."

They laughed and chatted as they packed up their knitting and headed out the door, even including Ivy in their conversation.

Standing at the counter, Melinda idly sorted through the handful of mail. Her hand froze when she discovered a letter from the head office of Montana Ranchers and Merchants Bank in Billings.

Her loan request.

She swallowed hard and stared at the envelope. Her hand shook.

"What's wrong?"

She looked up. Daniel had come to stand beside her and everyone else had left the shop.

"I think this letter is about my loan request."

"You planning to open it anytime soon? Or you just want to think the worst? It could be something about your identity having been stolen and you now owe them ten gazillion dollars. That'd be the worst, wouldn't it?"

She mock-glared at him. "I'll open it." Trembling on the inside, she ripped the flap off the envelope and slipped out the letter. Quickly, she read the bank's rejection of her request.

Disappointment weighed her shoulders down and brought stinging tears to her eyes that she refused to shed.

Daniel rested a consoling hand on her back. "They turned you down?"

"Looks like my idea to carry needlepoint merchandise will have to wait." She sniffed, then lifted her head. "As Ivy is so fond of saying, it's no big deal."

"Yeah, it is." He kneaded her neck with his fingers. "I'm sorry, Goldilocks."

She put the letter back on the counter. "So am I. But business is picking up. Another few months and maybe I can—"

He pulled her into his arms and held her. His warmth and strength flowed into her, and she rested her head on his shoulder. Safe, she thought. Secure. Loved.

Were her feelings for Daniel real? Did she deserve to love again? Live again? Could anything wipe away the guilt she'd carried for so long?

Forgive herself.

Ask the Lord.

Outside, Arnie gave the van's horn three short bursts.

Daniel let his hands slide down her arms and clasped her fingers. His dark brows pulled together to form a V and he looked into her eyes. "Big brother is getting restless."

"You'd better go."

"Are you going to be okay?"

A weak smile trembled at the corners of her lips. "Everyone has disappointments. I'll survive."

"Yes, you will." His words held so much confidence that she was tempted to believe him.

Believe in them together? That might be too much to ask or hope for.

Arnie honked again, louder this time.

"Gotta go." He kissed her, a fast peck that still had the power to speed up Melinda's heart rate.

Turning, Daniel jogged out the door and jumped into the van, automatically fastening his seat belt.

"About time." Arnie pulled the van away from the curb. "What took you two lovebirds so long?"

Lovebirds? Is that what he and Mindy were? "The bank turned down Mindy's request for a loan to expand the shop."

Arnie glanced at him. "Not much we can do about that."

"I might talk to Connolly at the bank. See what he says."

"Don't get carried away, bro. The O'Brien ranch isn't out of the woods yet. Your breeding scheme with Charlie hasn't produced a single foal yet and won't for months."

"I know." Daniel scooted down in the seat and stretched out his legs. There had to be something he could do to help Mindy out. Her look of abject despair had hit him right in the solar plexus like a mule kicking him in the gut. He felt as helpless as a heifer caught in spring flood and floating downstream fast.

But he couldn't do anything that would put the ranch at risk. That wouldn't be fair to Arnie.

Melinda closed up the shop and walked home to Aunt Martha's house.

If she could keep the knitting classes going

through the fall, she should be able to pay Daniel back his loan. Then maybe a few months after that she could start slow and bring in some needlepoint merchandise.

Maybe being the operative word.

She found Aunt Martha in the living room watching television and knitting.

"Hey, look at you," Melinda said. "You're knitting!" It looked like she was working on a child's wool cap for winter, one she'd give an organization that provided clothing for the poor.

Martha peered at her over the top of her glasses. "I've been knitting most of my life and now that young therapist of mine said I'd likely never get enough strength back in my hand to knit again."

"But you are!" Melinda was so tickled, she couldn't keep a smile off her face.

"I learned a long time ago just because somebody says something, that doesn't necessarily make it true." She shoved her glasses up on her nose and examined her knitting. "My stitches may not be the best I've ever done, but you can bet your last potato that they're a lot better than that young man could do."

Laughing, Melinda went into the kitchen to start dinner. Maybe, just maybe, she ought to rethink her business plan and have another chat with Richard Connolly at the bank. Potter Creek needed a knitting shop with a growing clientele. People shouldn't have to drive to Bozeman for a skein of yarn or supplies for their needlepoint project. Not when there was a perfectly good option right here in town.

She simply had to keep on trying.

Chapter Sixteen

On Sunday, Aunt Martha insisted she use her walker from the parking lot into church instead of being pushed in her wheelchair.

"What if your arms get too tired to hold you up?" Melinda asked. "Or worse, what if you fall?"

"Oh, pish-posh. I've been tramping around the house for weeks and haven't fallen yet. I'll be fine." She eased herself out of the Buick and firmly gripped her walker. "Besides, my therapist says I have to walk more or I'll end up an invalid in bed for the rest of my life. I have no intention of letting that happen."

Whatever the physical therapist had been telling Martha, she was certainly motivated these days.

Melinda stayed right beside Aunt Martha, ready to catch her if she fell. Belatedly, she realized she should get her aunt one of those walkers with wheels that could also be used as a chair. Then if Martha tired, she could sit and rest for a few minutes.

This afternoon or first thing tomorrow, Melinda

vowed to drive to the medical supply store in Boze-man and buy one.

Until that happened, she could only feel relieved when Daniel took up a position on the other side of her aunt. He was far stronger than she and better able to catch Martha if she faltered.

"Good morning, ladies," he said. "You're both look-ing exceptionally well this morning."

"Well is as well does," Martha replied tartly.

"It looks to me like you're getting ready for a foot race, Aunt Martha." Daniel looked past Martha and winked at Melinda.

"You bet I am, young man. I'm racing against old age and I plan to win." For emphasis, she kerthump-thumped her walker with more force than necessary.

Smiling to herself, she asked, "Where's Arnie this morning?"

"He had to come early for a meeting about the church budget," Daniel said. "He's good at crunching numbers and finding ways to save money."

Although Arnie had always been a serious, respon-sible kind of guy, she was amazed that both O'Brien brothers were so involved in church activities. They'd both gone through a lot of changes in the past ten years.

So had Melinda, not all of them good.

Inside the church, Daniel decided it would be easier for Aunt Martha to sit at the end of the pew rather than try to scoot down a few places. So Melinda entered first followed by Daniel, who then helped Aunt Martha. She sighed audibly when she sat down. That had been her longest walk since she got out of the hospital.

To Melinda's dismay, Daniel's thigh was pressed tightly against hers. She tried to slide down a few inches but a woman had made her way into the pew from the opposite side, trapping Melinda and giving her no room to move.

Her teeth on edge, her face flushed, she raised her eyes to the sharply pitched ceiling and prayed no one would notice how close they were sitting together.

When the congregation stood to sing the first hymn, Melinda practically elbowed the poor lady next to her out of the way to gain a few inches of space. Not that it helped much.

Daniel could be on the far side of the church, or in the next town, and she'd still sense his presence. Still know he had wheedled his way into her life and her heart. Just as he had ten years ago, and it terrified her just as much.

To add to her discomfort, the pastor's sermon was a about forgiving those who had sinned against you.

No one had sinned against Melinda. She'd done the worst all on her own.

Leaning even closer to her, Daniel whispered, "Have you talked to the pastor yet?"

She gave a quick shake of her head and kept her eyes riveted on Reverend Redmond standing behind the simple wooden pulpit.

"When we leave, you can catch Arthur at the door," Daniel said. "Ask him for an appointment."

She put her finger to her lips and shook her head

again. Confessing her sins to Daniel had been emotionally wrenching. She didn't want to go through that again anytime soon.

With the church service over, the three of them made their way up the aisle to the exit where Reverend Redmond stood greeting the members of the congregation.

Melinda considered making her escape via the side door, but she couldn't leave Aunt Martha on her own.

The pastor greeted Aunt Martha warmly, then turned to Melinda and took her hand in both of his. "Good to see you here this morning, Ms. Spencer. I'm sure your aunt feels fortunate that you are staying with her."

Melinda forced a smile. "I'm glad I can help her out." She eased her hand out of his grasp.

Snaring her arm so she couldn't step away, Daniel said, "Arthur, Melinda has been wanting to make an appointment to see you privately and talk. When would be a good time for you?"

The pastor's attention swiveled back to Melinda. "Why, I'd be happy to talk with you, Ms. Spencer. I have the afternoon free if you'd like to come by later."

Ready to throttle Daniel, she yanked her arm free. "I'm so sorry, Reverend. I have an errand and I have to run to Bozeman this afternoon. I'll call you to make arrangements."

"Then I'll look forward to hearing from you." Smiling politely, the preacher turned to the next person in line.

Melinda hurried away but hadn't gone far when Daniel caught up with her.

"Wait, Mindy. I was only trying to help."

She whirled on him. "You can help by not rushing me, O'Brien. If I want to talk to Reverend Redmond, I am perfectly capable of calling him myself."

Stalking off, she found Aunt Martha chatting with some friends and urged her to the car.

"Did you have a little spat with Daniel?" Martha asked as she eased herself into the Buick.

Melinda gritted her teeth. At the age of eighty-two, Martha's hearing was perfect and she rarely missed a thing.

"It was nothing to worry about," she said, hoping to reassure Martha.

And herself.

Daniel, riding April, and Arnie, maneuvering on his ATV, spent the afternoon moving twenty head of beef cattle to a separate pen where a truck would pick them up for shipment to the market in the morning. The payment they'd get for the cattle was the last piece of their balloon payment on the mortgage. After that it would be smooth sailing for the O'Brien ranch.

Assuming winter wasn't too harsh, killing off some of the herd, or a disease didn't hit the herd, wiping out the remaining cattle.

Montana ranching could be a risky business in the best of years.

After they cleaned up and had dinner, Daniel plopped down in his recliner and clicked on the TV. Not that he had any interest in the run-of-the-mill Sunday evening shows.

He was far too worried about Mindy and her reluctance to talk with Pastor Redmond.

Arnie rolled his chair into the living room. "What's on tonight?"

"Nothing worth seeing."

Picking up a magazine, Arnie flipped through the pages. "You've been pretty quiet since church this morning. What's going on?"

Daniel glanced over his shoulder. "It's Mindy. She still hasn't talked to the pastor."

"Why is she dragging her feet?"

"Who knows. She's so knotted up with this guilt business, she can't let it go." If he could, Daniel would drag her kicking and screaming to talk with the reverend. But he'd obviously stepped over a line when he'd tried to force her into making an appointment with the pastor. Despite her innocent appearance and sweet smile, she was one strong, independent woman.

"Have you tried telling her how you feel?"

Daniel snapped the footrest down and turned to Arnie. "What do you mean, how I feel?"

"You've had the look of a man in love since she showed up in town."

"I have not!" Daniel's Adam's apple bounced on the lie.

Shrugging, Arnie tossed the magazine back onto the end table. "I don't know many guys who would take up knitting to please a woman."

"I didn't want her business to fail right off and the kids needed a service project. What's the matter with that?"

"Not a thing. But maybe if you told her you love her, she'd figure out a way to put the past behind her so the two of you could get married."

"I can't do that."

"Why not? You won't know how she feels about you unless you take the plunge first. Women are like that. They want to know you're serious about them."

Snapping off the TV, Daniel stood and walked to the window. Darkness was falling fast. The barn and horse pasture were in deep shadow now and only a fine line in the western sky revealed the last traces of the setting sun.

"If I told her how I feel, she'd start thinking about marriage. Women are like that, too, and I'm not going to get married."

He waited for Arnie to say something. Instead his comment was met with silence.

Finally, Daniel turned around. "I'm not going to marry her because you've got this fool idea that you'd be a third wheel and you'd have to move out of the house. That's not going to happen, bro."

"Fine. Some other guy will," Arnie said. "How does that sound?"

A sharp pain slammed into Daniel's chest.

Arnie's lips twitched. "We'll work it out, bro. *If* Melinda is dumb enough to marry you."

By Monday morning, Aunt Martha had mastered her new walker and Melinda was ready to confront Richard Connolly at the bank with a new business plan and her request for a line of credit. She'd drawn pie charts and graphs. She'd projected income, expenses and cash flow.

She'd all but inked the plan in her own blood.

Leaving the house earlier than usual, she went to the bank and walked directly to Connolly's desk. He was on the phone but he gestured for her to take the leather chair she'd sat in last time.

Melinda elected to remain standing. This time around, she wanted to be in the power position.

"I apologize for not calling for an appointment," she said when he'd finished his call. "But I won't take up much of your time."

He stood. "If you're here because headquarters rejected your loan request, I'm afraid there isn't much—"

"I don't give up that easily, Mr. Connolly. I'm here because I've revised my request. My business plan is solid and your bank would be foolish not to extend Aunt Martha's Knitting and Notions a line of credit that would benefit the community."

She handed him the new proposal. "I anticipate when my plan is fully implemented I will be able to employ a part-time employee, which will generate more income to support other local businesses when that person spends her paycheck in town. I assume you're aware that small businesses are the growth engine for our economy."

"Well, yes. That's true." Sounding flustered by her approach, he looked down at the folder she'd handed him.

"Excellent. Then I will expect a favorable recommendation from you and will look forward to hearing from you soon." She nodded once. "Thank you for your time."

With that, she turned and walked out of the bank. Her knees were shaking so badly that as soon as she was out of sight, she leaned against the building and gulped a deep breath of fresh air.

This time she would not fail.

After getting the twenty head of beef cattle loaded for shipment to market, Daniel cleaned up and headed for town.

It was midafternoon when he got to the bank. Mindy was determined to make the knitting shop a success. If he helped her, she'd realize how much he cared. The past and her feelings of guilt wouldn't steamroller her at every turn. She could look to the future—*their* future—and move forward.

Before he stepped into the bank he said a silent prayer. *God, I'd appreciate it if You could help me out here. This is important and I don't want to mess it up. Thanks.*

Pulling open the door, he stepped inside and headed for Richard Connolly's desk.

"Hey, Richard. How's it going?"

Connolly stood and extended his hand. "Can't complain. How about you?"

"I'm here to take care of the mortgage payment on the ranch."

"Terrific. Sit down and I'll get the paperwork together."

Daniel signed over the check for the sale of the cattle

and transferred money from the ranch account to pay the remainder due.

Connolly entered the data in his computer, gave copies of the forms to Daniel, then sat back in his chair. "You and your brother are to be congratulated. Frankly, when your father died, I thought the two of you would blow the ranch off and leave town. Instead, you've turned the ranch around and it's a showpiece. You both can feel very proud of what you've accomplished."

"Thanks. We're glad to have that monkey off our backs." As proud as Daniel felt, he wanted Mindy to experience the same success. "There's something else I wanted to talk with you about."

"If it's another loan, I'm pretty sure headquarters will approve it. Your credit is good with us."

"That's not exactly what I had in mind."

Connolly's eyes widened and he scratched his chin thoughtfully as Daniel explained that he wanted to guarantee Mindy's loan.

"But I don't want Mindy to know that I provided the collateral and cosigned for her loan. I want the success of the shop to be hers, not mine."

"Are you sure? You're taking a substantial risk. If her shop fails…"

"It won't." Daniel had complete faith in Mindy and her business sense.

What he didn't know was how she would react if and when she learned he had cosigned her loans.

That was a risk he didn't want to take.

Chapter Seventeen

For the second time since dinner, Melinda got up from the couch, walked into the kitchen and couldn't remember why she was there.

With a sigh, she returned to the living room. All day she'd jumped when the shop door opened as though she expected the entire staff of Montana Ranchers and Merchants Bank to come trooping in to announce she wasn't worthy. No loan for her. Not even a line of credit.

Aunt Martha looked up from her knitting. "You're very restless this evening, dear."

"I took the new business plan into the bank this morning."

"What did Richard say?"

"Not much. I didn't give him a chance."

"Come sit down, dear. Let's talk."

Melinda hated to trouble her aunt. She was the one who had volunteered to manage the shop. She had bragged that she was capable of doing the job. So far she hadn't lived up to her own hype.

She slumped down on the couch again. A reality show was on television, but the sound had been turned down. Melinda's own reality seemed to consist of one disaster after another.

"Tell me, what is the worst thing that can happen if you don't get the money?" her aunt asked.

"If I don't get the approval I'll have to struggle along with only knitting supplies until I can build up enough cash to buy some needlepoint inventory."

"You'd still be able to manage the shop, wouldn't you?"

"Well, yes, but it should be bringing in more money. I want to draw customers from a wider area. People who'd rather shop in Potter Creek than go to Bozeman. I want to be the Johnny Appleseed of knitting and needlepoint."

"Even if you aren't able to expand just yet, we'd still have a roof over our heads. Food in the cupboard."

"All of which you're providing. I'm supposed to be here helping you, not the other way around."

Her aunt's smile was that of an aging angel, wrinkled and sweet and comforting. "My dear, you bring me great joy simply by being here."

That didn't seem like nearly enough to Melinda. She'd had great hopes for her future when she came to Potter Creek.

"When I was a young woman," Martha said, "I learned that if I spent my life worrying about things I couldn't change, then I'd miss the joy of living in the here and now. There's a Bible verse that helps me remember not to fret about tomorrow. I'm sure you're familiar with the verse."

She took off her glasses and looked off into the distance as though recalling the time and place when she'd committed the verse to memory. "Jesus said, 'Therefore I tell you, do not worry about your life, what you will eat or drink; or about your body, what you will wear. Is not life more important than food, and the body more important than clothes? Look at the birds of the air; they do not sow or reap or store away in barns, and yet your heavenly Father feeds them. Are you not much more valuable than they? Who of you by worrying can add a single hour to his life?'"

"I hope that means God is going to cosign the credit application?" Just once, Melinda wished God would be on her side.

Martha chuckled. "Not literally, I don't imagine. I am sure, however, that we can leave the outcome in God's hands."

Melinda certainly hoped her aunt was right.

By the time Grace and Ivy showed up prior to knitting class, Melinda had pretty well adjusted to letting life happen. As Aunt Martha had said, there wasn't much use in worrying over things you couldn't change.

She sat down between the two girls. "Ivy, it looks to me that using ten-and-a-half size straight needles and a circular needle in that same size will work best for your design."

"Circular needle?" Ivy echoed. "What's that?"

Grace popped up and brought an example to the

table. "There's a video on YouTube that shows you how to use one. It's kind of cool, really."

Melinda smiled to herself. Amazing how Ivy's artistic skills, once revealed, bought her a lot of cachet with the younger teens. She seemed to be beaming from the inside out these days.

The rest of the class members wandered in and settled around the table. Daniel arrived a little late. Melinda made it a point not to look at him. She still hadn't called Pastor Redmond and didn't plan to. Yet, anyway.

She noted Arnie wasn't with him, and wondered where his brother was.

"Has everyone finished their squares?" she asked, focusing on the teenagers, not their leader.

"I haven't," Dwayne admitted. "My dad's got me painting the barn this summer."

The teens groaned on his behalf.

"Would you like someone to finish the square for you?"

The boy glanced at his friends. "Naw, I'll get it done. I want to be able to sign the card like the rest of these guys."

Patti said, "I've been gone for a week visiting my aunt in Spokane, and I forgot to take my knitting with me."

"I bet her dog ate her homework, too," Frank teased.

Patti punched his shoulder. "Oh, hush!"

"I brought in Arnie's square. He had to go into Bozeman this afternoon." Daniel tossed it on the table. "I finished mine, too." A second square landed by the first.

The kids cheered, and a shiver of pleasure raised gooseflesh down her spine. The big macho cowboy had come through for her and the teenagers. The quirky grin on his face said he was proud of himself and she agreed.

Becca said, "Because there's plenty of summer left, I'm going to knit some more squares. Maybe we should be doing more squares for another lap robe for a wounded warrior?"

The boys objected, Frank saying, "Can't we do some other service project? Like mow somebody's lawn or paint an old lady's house?"

"You guys can do what you want, but once I'm done with the barn, I'm through with painting," Dwayne said.

"Let's talk about a new project at our next meeting," Daniel suggested. "Everybody can come up with ideas and we'll take a vote."

The teenagers seemed content with Daniel's plan, although some of the girls wanted to knit additional squares during the coming week.

Except for Daniel, the group began to break up. He lingered behind. "It sounded like the majority of the kids want to pick a different service project for the rest of the summer," Daniel said.

"I think we'll have enough accomplished to send off two lap robes, and that's fine. Grace and Ivy are definitely hooked on knitting now, too. They'll be regular customers." She straightened some of the craft show flyers on the counter. "You getting the youth group involved in the lap robe project really helped out the shop."

"I'm glad." Acting as though he was about to leave, he picked up his Stetson and settled it on his head.

The door behind him opened. To Melinda's surprise, Mr. Connolly from the bank stepped inside.

Her stomach sank. Was he delivering the bank's rejection letter personally this time?

"Hello, you two." He nodded to Daniel and gave Melinda a warm smile. "I have some good news for you, young lady."

She held her breath and mentally crossed her fingers.

"The Billings office has approved your line of credit. Congratulations, Ms. Spencer."

Her heart leaped into her throat. Tears of relief glazed her eyes. Bringing her hands together in a prayerful manner, she looked heavenward. "Thank you, Lord."

Connolly laughed and slapped Daniel on the back. "In this case, the thanks ought to go to this cowboy."

"Richard," Daniel said in a warning tone.

"Oh, right…" Connolly straightened his shirt cuffs before handing Melinda an envelope. "Come in during the next day or two and we'll set up the account."

Looking from Connolly, whose face had flushed, to Daniel, who was frowning at the banker, Melinda detected a strange undercurrent flowing between the two men. A spark of intuition started a slow burn in her chest.

"Why should I thank Daniel, Mr. Connolly?" She

spoke each word slowly. Distinctly. "Did he have something to do with my getting the line of credit approved?"

"You have a great business plan, Mindy," Daniel said.

"Mr. Connolly, I directed that question to you."

Connolly's gaze flitted around the shop as though looking for a place for him to hide. Self-consciously, he rubbed the side of his nose. "Daniel's right. Good business plan. I'm confident you'll be successful." He backed up a few steps. "Drop by the bank soon."

He fled out the door leaving Melinda staring at Daniel, suspicion crawling up her neck like an army of ants.

She folded her right arm across her chest, grabbing her left elbow, and tapped the unopened envelope against her thigh. "You did something, didn't you?"

"Hey, I don't know what you're talking about." He held his arms out wide, his palms toward her, looking everywhere except right at her. "You got what you wanted. You can expand your inventory. That's great. You should be jumping around, happy as a puppy with a new bone."

Why was he looking so guilty? Had he blackmailed Connolly to get him to give Melinda the line of credit? Threatened him?

"Aren't you going to open the letter?" Daniel asked, a plea in his voice.

She already knew, basically, what the letter would say. So did Daniel. He'd recently paid off his mortgage.

Her eyes widened. Her credit was good at the bank.

Surprise and shock tangled with her conscience. "You guaranteed my credit line, didn't you? You used your ranch as collateral. Daniel, how could you risk your ranch for some needlepoint supplies?"

Taking off his hat, he thrust his fingers through his hair. "I didn't mortgage the ranch."

"Then what? What did you use for collateral?"

A muscle ticked in his jaw. "A horse."

Horse. Singular. She cocked her head and lowered her brows, narrowing her eyes. "Which horse?"

"What does it matter? You're going to pay the money back. I'm not going to lose anything."

"Oh, my…" Her body remained still as she processed what he must have done. "For collateral, you used April!"

He stepped forward. "I did it for us, Goldilocks."

"For *us?*" She retreated behind the counter. "You risked your prize horse for *us?* The horse you and Charlie Moffett are going to breed so you can make the big bucks?" Her voice rose in pitch, straining the muscles of her throat. "I don't get it."

"I know how much you want the shop to be successful. I thought… I mean, I wanted to help you out because I think you and I, the two of us…" His shoulders sagged. He looked down at the floor as though looking for a trapdoor and stuffed his hands in his pockets. When he lifted his head, he met her gaze straight on and said, "Because I think the two of us could have a future together."

Together. Her thoughts began to soar. The forbidden

dream hers for the taking. It would be as though the past ten years had never happened. No husband. No son.

Nooo, a voice screamed in her head.

She began breathing too hard. The icy claws of panic scraped over her skin. Beneath her flesh a wave of anger fought to escape, drowning the tiny spark of hope that had so briefly flared.

She made small, choking noises in her throat. Dreams didn't come true.

"You didn't believe I could get a line of credit on my own merit."

"They had turned you down, Mindy. I have faith in you. That's why I signed the guarantee. For you. For us."

The envelope in her hand quivered like the leaves of a quaking aspen in a high wind. By changing her loan request to a line of credit, she'd been so sure she'd get the bank's approval. Apparently it took more than just her signature.

She ripped open the envelope and read the letter. The words were those she had hoped to see: approval, line of credit, ten thousand dollars, moderate interest rate due on the money withdrawn. But none of the words were her doing.

Daniel had risked April, the basis for his partnership with Charlie.

She couldn't accept that risk.

Carefully, she ripped the letter in half once and then again, letting the scraps of white paper flutter into the trash can behind the counter.

"Why did you do that?" he asked.

"You had no right to gamble on me. No right to put your livelihood in jeopardy and risk April."

His face darkened like the clouds of an approaching storm. He squinted, his eyes nailing her in place. His black stare bored into her, making her heart hammer and her veins constrict. His fingers flexed into fists.

"You're convinced nothing good will ever happen to you, aren't you?"

She didn't answer. She didn't think she could. Her vocal cords had gone rigid along with her spine.

"Maybe you're right," he continued. "Or maybe you just like being a victim."

He whirled, flung open the door and stalked out of the shop.

Like fragile glass, Melinda's heart shattered, the slivered shards slicing and carving, opening old scars that had never healed. Silently, she slipped to the floor where she curled herself into the fetal position.

"Please, God. Help me."

Chapter Eighteen

That evening at dinner, Melinda sat idly running her fingertip over the chrome band around the kitchen table. Cold to the touch. Featureless.

Years of pain and loss had hollowed her out, leaving only an empty shell. Nothing stirred inside her. No thought. No emotion. No dreams. Cold.

"Mindy, dear," Aunt Martha said. "You're not eating your dinner. Are you all right?"

"I'm fine." Her voice sounded as flat and colorless as a cracked church bell in a faraway steeple.

"You don't look well. You're pale. Are you coming down with something?"

Looking up, Melinda shook her head. She picked up her fork, but the thought of eating anything roiled her stomach.

"May I ask you a personal question, Aunt Martha?"

"Of course." Martha's appetite appeared much better

than Melinda's, her chicken salad with walnuts and goat cheese almost gone. "What would you like to know?"

"I've seen pictures of you as a young woman. You were very attractive. Why didn't you ever marry?"

"Oh, my..." Martha blinked several times, then smiled one of those I'm-remembering-something-special smiles. "I came close once. His name was Kurt Huhn. He was German and had been in a prisoner of war camp north of here. When World War II ended, he decided not to go home. He was working as a ranch hand. He was so very handsome. Blond. Tall. And such a gentleman. I'm afraid I was quite taken with him."

Pausing, Martha took a sip of her iced tea. "I was only seventeen. He was twenty-four. My parents were set against him. You see, they were loyal Americans, very patriotic, and the war had been hard on our GIs overseas. Many of the boys from around here didn't come home."

"War is hard on both sides," Melinda commented, fascinated by her great-aunt's story.

"Oh, yes. And Kurt had lost his entire family. Two brothers, his parents and a younger sister. But he harbored no hard feelings toward us."

Empathy for all of those who had been lost, and for the survivors, tugged at corners of Melinda's conscience.

"He wanted us to run away together. Move to California. But I didn't want to go against my parents' wishes. You see, I thought if they got to know Kurt better, they'd come to love him, too.

"But the mood in Montana right after the war was

very anti-German, particularly as the GIs who had survived the war began to return home. Some of the young men were upset that Kurt was courting me. One night—" Martha's voice caught and she blinked again. "On a Saturday night he went into town with some of the other ranch hands. No one ever admitted exactly what happened. Kurt was found the next morning." Her chin trembled and she covered her mouth with her hand. "He'd been beaten to death."

"Oh, Aunt Martha. How terrible. You must've been brokenhearted."

"I was. I cried for a week. Not only because he'd been killed but also because I blamed myself for his death."

Melinda gaped at her aunt. "It wasn't your fault Kurt was killed."

"Not directly, no. But if he hadn't been seeing me. Or if I'd run away with him as he had asked, he wouldn't have died. Rational or not, I felt as guilty as if I'd killed him myself."

Just as Melinda carried the guilt of killing her husband and her child.

Stunned, she tried to shake the cobwebs from her mind. "How did you get past feeling guilty?"

"I didn't for a very long time. I stayed by myself. I never went out with my friends. I barely spoke to anyone. If it hadn't been against God's laws, I might have taken my own life."

"I'm so glad you didn't, Aunt Martha."

She smiled. "So am I, my dear. Fortunately, after a time I began to realize Kurt wouldn't have wanted me to waste away the rest of my life. But I was never able to find a man who I could love as much as I loved Kurt, and that may be because I had turned him into more than an ordinary man. In my imagination, he was the perfect mate. None other would do. I'd placed dear Kurt on a pedestal. But I did begin to live my life more fully, and for that I'm grateful."

Rubbing her temple, Melinda wondered at the terrible loss Aunt Martha had experienced. Not only had she lost the man she'd loved, but she had also forgone any chance of loving again or having a family of her own. What a tragedy.

She stopped the mindless rubbing of her temple. Was she making the same mistake that her aunt had? Refusing a chance for love and the future by remaining chained to the past?

By remaining a victim?

But how could she unlock those chains? She couldn't simply forget Joe and what she'd forced him to do. She could never, ever forget Jason. Nor could she forget her guilt or the weight of that heavy burden.

For the rest of the week, Melinda vacillated between anger at Daniel for risking his favorite horse for her and desperately wanting to see him. Why had he been willing to risk his favorite horse? She didn't want to be indebted to him.

She dropped stitches every time she tried to knit and didn't discover her error until three rows later.

When she caught a glimpse of herself in a mirror, her complexion looked like yarn that had been bleached gray and the bags under her eyes had turned her into a raccoon.

The teenagers came to class with enough completed squares to make three lap robes. She showed them how to weave the squares together with matching yarn.

They all signed the poster-board cards Ivy had made, bright, colorful cartoon characters of soldiers with bandaged heads, missing legs, broken bodies and brave smiles on their faces. Inside the message was a bold THANK YOU.

Daniel wasn't there to sign his name or write a message.

Melinda promised to wash, package and mail the afghans to the Army Wounded Warrior project at Walter Reed Hospital in Washington, D.C.

With a smile as fragile as papier-mâché, she hugged the kids goodbye, told them to drop by anytime.

On the inside, the ache near her heart immobilized the flow of blood to her brain.

She couldn't think.

Her lungs constricted.

She couldn't draw a breath.

She loved Daniel. She'd never stopped loving him.

On Sunday, she looked for Daniel. He wasn't in church. She'd hurt him and driven him away, just as she'd driven Joe away by ignoring his needs and concentrating on Jason.

When the service was over, Melinda stood beside her aunt as Martha thanked Reverend Redmond and shook his hand.

"As always, Pastor, your sermon was inspiring," Martha said. "Though truth be told, at my age I'm not looking for the door of opportunity to open. I'm more interested in making sure heaven's door opens when I knock."

"You never know, Martha." An amused smile laced the pastor's voice with good humor. "They tell me it's never too late for opportunity to knock, and I don't think heaven's ready for you just yet."

She patted the pastor's hand and stepped away, leaving Reverend Redmond's full attention directed at Melinda.

"How are you, young lady?" he asked, closing both his hands around hers.

"I'm, um…I need help," she stammered. "Could you—"

"I'll be in my office this afternoon at three, if you'd like."

She gave an affirmative nod and quickly hurried after her aunt. Her knees were weak, her mouth dry. Impending tears burned and the dark shadow of panic threatened to overtake her.

She could call and cancel the appointment.

Or not show up.

She could be a victim for the rest of her life.

Or she could dare to live her life.

Going to see the minister was worse than the time Melinda had been called into the principal's office for setting off firecrackers to signal the beginning of senior ditch day. She'd thought at the time he might not let her graduate.

Now she was afraid Reverend Redmond would condemn her for what she had done to her husband and son.

After eating lunch with Aunt Martha, Melinda drove back to the church. She flicked on the car radio. All she could find was country-and-western music and she wasn't in the mood.

The fingers of one hand fluttered against the steering wheel like the wings of a moth trying to escape a spiderweb.

She rolled down the car window and let the hot summer air blow in her face. That did little to tame the chills that raised goose bumps on her arms.

The church office was located adjacent to the community meeting room. She parked and followed the flower-lined path to the door. She hesitated, then lifted her chin before turning the knob and stepping inside.

No one was in the church secretary's outer office, the desk cleared of everything except a pen holder and family pictures.

"Come on in, Melinda," the pastor called from his adjoining office as he came to meet her. He'd removed the jacket he'd worn for the morning service but still wore a short-sleeve navy T-shirt and his clerical collar. "I'm glad you came."

Her urge to flee nearly drove her back out the door. "Thank you for seeing me on such short notice." Her voice quavered.

"My pleasure. I had hoped we'd have a chance to get

acquainted." He ushered her into his office and indicated a grouping of comfortable chairs by the window. A poplar tree stood in the lawn outside the window, the leaves as still as in a painting.

She sat down, smoothed her skirt over her legs and folded her hands together to keep them from shaking.

The minister sat opposite her, leaning back comfortably. A gentle smile played at the corners of his lips and his hazel eyes spoke of kindness.

"How have you enjoyed your stay in Potter Creek so far?" he asked.

She cleared the lump from her throat. "Fine."

"Some of the young people have told me how much they've enjoyed learning to knit. And the project you've had them working on is excellent. Our wounded warriors need all the help and support we can give them."

"Yes, sir. The young people have done a fine job. They're nice kids, all of them."

He nodded. "Then you're not here to report their misbehavior?"

Melinda sputtered in surprise. "Oh, no, not at all. They've been wonderful to work with."

"Good. Then why don't you tell me why you wanted to talk with me? You seem quite distressed." He leaned forward, his elbows resting on the arms of his chair, his hands relaxed, his gaze fixed on her.

"I, um, I'm not quite sure how to describe the problem."

"That's all right. We're in no rush. Why don't you simply start at the beginning."

Melinda searched her mind to find the origins of her

guilt, the sins that had caused her so much pain. Perhaps the first misstep had been when she married Joe even when she still harbored forbidden feelings for Daniel, the baddest bad boy she had ever met.

She told the pastor about her marriage, the first two years, years that were happy, and how they decided to start a family. She was sure a child would bring them closer together, and Jason had.

Reverend Redmond nodded as she spoke and made small encouraging sounds that prompted her to continue.

"Then, a few weeks after Jason turned two, things changed…"

As she continued, the pastor handed her a box of tissues to wipe the tears she hadn't realized were falling. He handed her a bottle of water. She took a big gulp, almost choking before she could go on.

By the time she told him about holding Jason in her arms for the last time, the shadow of the poplar tree had lengthened and shifted like a sundial.

She wiped her eyes again. "I feel so guilty."

"Let's talk about that for a moment," the pastor said. "Did you love your husband?"

"Yes. Perhaps not as passionately as I should have."

"Did he love you?"

"Yes," she whispered.

Leaning back in his chair, the pastor tented his fingers. "You know, men are strange creatures. We don't know how to nurture the way women do. When there's a child as sick as Jason was, we feel helpless." His voice even, nonjudgmental, he studied Melinda intently. "Did it occur to you that you didn't drive Joe away? Instead, by going to Afghanistan he chose to do the only thing he knew how to do to help his family."

Melinda fussed with the damp tissue in her hand. Something niggled at the back of her mind as though a door inside had been pushed open a crack letting in a sliver of light.

"No, I hadn't thought of it in that way." She'd experienced resentment that he'd left her alone, anger that he'd gotten himself blown up and finally guilt that it was her fault.

"That's all right. Give it some thought over the next few days." He gave her a moment to absorb what he'd said. "Now about Jason. I don't imagine there is a greater grief than losing a child. It doesn't seem natural that a child should die before his parents, yet it happens all too many times."

She nodded. Knowing that was true changed nothing.

"Tell me, by the time Jason slipped into a coma, was there anything at all you or the doctors could have done to save him."

"I prayed." Her throat threatened to close down tight. "God didn't hear me."

"I believe He did hear you, Melinda. I can't tell you why He needed Jason to be by His side, but I do know your son is safe in Heaven and waiting for you when your time comes."

A sob escaped her throat.

"For whatever sins you may have committed, God

has long since forgiven you. Now you only have to forgive yourself."

"But how? I can't simply forget my husband and son."

"Of course not. When the Lord forgives our sins, it doesn't mean He forgets them. It means He chooses not to bring up our sins in a negative way. Your marriage, your child, were blessings from God. Remember them in that way."

He leaned forward and covered her hand. "Do you think you can do that, Melinda?"

Her chest ached, and her eyes burned. "I don't know. I simply don't know."

Chapter Nineteen

Daniel spent the better part of Friday checking fences. As he rode back to the ranch house, he was hot, tired and hungry.

Dismounting, he led April to the trough for a well-earned drink. He dropped the reins, hung his hat on the saddle horn and dunked his head in the sun-warmed water. He came up sputtering. Water dripped from his hair and he gave his head a shake like a dog after a dip in a creek.

More than a week since he'd seen Mindy and he couldn't get her out of his head no matter how hard he drove himself. If this kept up, he'd have to talk to Pastor Redmond. Or see a shrink.

The sound of an approaching car drew his attention. He finger combed his wet hair and squinted down the drive. An old, silver Buick sedan stirred up a dust tail as it crept toward the ranch house.

His heart lunged against his ribs. Anger and elation

wrestled each other for supremacy. Fear and relief held their own match and came to a draw.

He strolled out to meet the car. Mindy got out and stood behind the open door, using it as a shield. Or maybe she wanted to make a quick escape.

"Hi," she said, the word soft, tentative, as though she didn't know what else to say.

Neither did he. "Hi, yourself." He kept walking until only a few feet and the shield of steel separated them. She had on a sleeveless blouse, and her bare arms were smooth, lightly tanned.

"The lap robes are all ready to be shipped to the military hospital in D.C. I thought because you're the one who got the kids involved, you'd like to sign the cards. Ivy designed them."

She'd driven out here for that? She could've called, asked him to come into the shop. Or to her house. Or forgotten it altogether.

"Sure, I'll sign them."

Retrieving the cards from the backseat, she stepped around the open door to put them on the hood of the car. "I brought a pen for you."

When she looked up, her eyes were a deep blue, reflecting the sky. She looked younger, somehow, and the shadows that had haunted her seemed to have faded.

He took the pen and smiled as he saw the cartoon characters on the front of the cards. "Ivy's good, isn't she?"

"She has a God-given talent she's been hiding all

these years. I think she's going to start using that talent now."

He skimmed the notes the kids had written, added his own. On the back of the card, in fine calligraphy, Ivy had indicated the afghan was made by the youth group of Potter Creek Community Church and included the address. Maybe the kids would get a thank-you letter or two.

As he signed the third card, Melinda said, "I talked with Reverend Redmond last Sunday."

His head came up slowly. His heart stilled.

"I've been praying hard all week. I'm not all the way there yet, but I'm working on it. I don't want to be a victim, Daniel. I want a second chance to live my life."

Not knowing quite what to expect, he turned to face her.

"I wanted you to see a picture of Jason." She slipped a snapshot from her pocket and handed it to him. "It's the only picture I brought with me to Montana. The scrapbooks are stored at a friend's house in Pittsburgh. I'm going to send for them."

"Cute kid." Blond like his mom with a wicked twinkle in his blue eyes. A kid who would be hard not to love. Harder to lose. "I'm sorry you lost him."

"I'll never forget Jason. He'll always have a special place in my heart. And Joe, too. But I'm trying to set aside my grief and my guilt and remember the joy we had together."

"That's good. Remembering the joy."

The tip of her tongue swept across her lips. "Daniel,

if you're still interested, if you think it's still possible, I'd like us to be together, too. The truth is, a part of me never forgot you. Or stopped loving you."

His knees went as weak as a newborn colt. He wrapped his arms around her as much to hold her as to keep himself upright.

"Oh, man, I thought I'd lost you again. I love you, Goldilocks. I think maybe I always did."

She lifted her head and kissed him. Her kiss filled him with her sweetness and her promise. It filled him with her love and her hope for their future.

In return, he poured his heart out, silently vowing to be the best man he could be. For her. Always for her.

They married the following spring when the poplar tree at the church was bright green with fresh shoots.

With a look of delight on his face, Reverend Arthur Redmond officiated. Arnie, dressed in a Western-style tuxedo, served as Daniel's best man.

Ivy, who would be attending the College of Arts and Architecture in Bozeman in the fall on scholarship, wore a bridesmaid's outfit she'd designed herself. In the sleek print dress with a bolero jacket over a sleeveless top, she looked like a young princess from some exotic country.

She'd designed Melinda's dress, as well, a light blue skirt of silk that flowed around her knees and a hand-knitted top with cap sleeves that hugged her bodice. The bouquet of cut flowers she carried included two white roses in memory of Joe and Jason.

The church was nearly full as Aunt Martha, radiant

in a lace gown and holding Melinda's arm, escorted the bride down the aisle.

"He's almost as handsome as my Kurt was," she whispered in Melinda's ear.

"I wish you'd been able to marry Kurt."

"I missed my chance, dear. I'm glad you were not that foolish."

As Melinda looked at the man waiting for her in front of the altar, she knew the Lord had had a hand in bringing her back to Potter Creek and Daniel. She still didn't understand why the Lord had taken her son. She'd ask Him when He called her to His side.

Until then she'd live her life loving Daniel and pray that the Lord would grant her another child to hold in her arms.

* * * * *

Dear Reader,

In this story, Melinda had suffered two major losses, her husband and subsequently her son. I cannot imagine the pain of losing anyone I love, much less a child.

As *Big Sky Reunion* opens, Jason has been dead for about six months. Grief is a very personal pain. It can't be calibrated in days or months; we all experience grief in different ways.

One of my favorite organizations is Hospice. Almost every community across the country has a Hospice program that helps families deal with loved ones who are dying or have died. If you have experienced a loss— even if your loved one wasn't part of the Hospice program—they can help you deal with your grief. Most large hospitals also have grief counseling programs, which I strongly recommend. Your church may also have a similar program.

Melinda's grief, understandably, is referred to in Hospice literature as "complicated" grief. She was preoccupied with guilt and self-reproach. She is not alone. Nor are others who are having trouble, in their grief, experiencing sleep disturbance, lack of emotions, uncontrolled anger or a whole rash of other emotions that seem out of control.

If you're dealing with grief, I urge you to contact your local Hospice organization, a nearby hospital or your pastor for help.

To say grief can be a debilitating experience is an understatement. Ask for help. From God and from those who understand what you are experiencing.

Best wishes,
Charlotte Carter

QUESTIONS FOR DISCUSSION

1. If you have experienced the loss of a loved one, what helped you the most to deal with your grief?

2. What organizations in your community offer grief counseling?

3. What do you remember the most about your high school boyfriend? Would you like to go back and relive those years? Why or why not?

4. As teenagers, the characters in this book hung out at a riverside park. Where did your teenage crowd hang out?

5. What do you think are the best—and worst—parts of growing up in a small town?

6. Did you ever spend a summer living with relatives on a farm, a ranch or in a small town? Was it fun?

7. Have you ever gone back to the town where you grew up? Did you find the people or the place much different than you remembered? In what ways was it different or the same?

8. What would be the hardest for you to adjust to, moving from a small town to a city or moving from a city to a small town? Why?

9. Do you have any relatives or friends serving in the Middle East? How do you keep in touch?

10. Is there a particular craft you enjoy—sewing, quilting, painting, knitting, crocheting, woodworking, scrapbooking or something else? What makes this craft so enjoyable for you?

11. Do you enjoy horseback riding? English or Western saddle? Why?

12. Does your church host an annual craft show or bazaar as a fundraiser? In what way do you participate?

13. The characters in this book are attending a Potato Festival. What festivals do you enjoy attending in your community?

14. Some marriage proposals are quite romantic. If you are married, where were you when your husband proposed? Had he arranged a special location or event for his proposal?

15. The church youth group in this story made lap robes for wounded soldiers. Have you ever knitted, crocheted or sewn items for a charitable group? Do you find that effort fulfilling?

If you or your friends are interested in making lap robes for wounded soldiers, contact:
http://soldiersangels.org/blankets-of-gratitude.html

INSPIRATIONAL

Inspirational romances to warm your heart & soul.

TITLES AVAILABLE NEXT MONTH

Available May 31, 2011

SECOND CHANCE DAD
Aspen Creek Crossroads
Roxanne Rustand

ROCKY POINT REUNION
Barbara McMahon

AN ACCIDENTAL FAMILY
Accidental Blessings
Loree Lough

THE COWBOY'S HOMECOMING
Brenda Minton

HOME SWEET HOME
Kim Watters

SMALL-TOWN HEARTS
Men of Allegany County
Ruth Logan Herne

REQUEST YOUR FREE BOOKS!

2 FREE INSPIRATIONAL NOVELS
PLUS 2
FREE
MYSTERY GIFTS

YES! Please send me 2 FREE Love Inspired® novels and my 2 FREE mystery gifts (gifts are worth about $10). After receiving them, if I don't wish to receive any more books, I can return the shipping statement marked "cancel." If I don't cancel, I will receive 6 brand-new novels every month and be billed just $4.24 per book in the U.S. or $4.74 per book in Canada. That's a saving of at least 23% off the cover price. It's quite a bargain! Shipping and handling is just 50¢ per book in the U.S. and 75¢ per book in Canada.* I understand that accepting the 2 free books and gifts places me under no obligation to buy anything. I can always return a shipment and cancel at any time. Even if I never buy another book, the two free books and gifts are mine to keep forever.

105/305 IDN FDA5

Name	(PLEASE PRINT)	
Address		Apt. #
City	State/Prov.	Zip/Postal Code

Signature (if under 18, a parent or guardian must sign)

Mail to the **Reader Service:**
IN U.S.A.: P.O. Box 1867, Buffalo, NY 14240-1867
IN CANADA: P.O. Box 609, Fort Erie, Ontario L2A 5X3

Not valid for current subscribers to Love Inspired books.

**Are you a subscriber to Love Inspired books
and want to receive the larger-print edition?
Call 1-800-873-8635 or visit www.ReaderService.com.**

* Terms and prices subject to change without notice. Prices do not include applicable taxes. Sales tax applicable in N.Y. Canadian residents will be charged applicable taxes. Offer not valid in Quebec. This offer is limited to one order per household. All orders subject to credit approval. Credit or debit balances in a customer's account(s) may be offset by any other outstanding balance owed by or to the customer. Please allow 4 to 6 weeks for delivery. Offer available while quantities last.

Your Privacy—The Reader Service is committed to protecting your privacy. Our Privacy Policy is available online at www.ReaderService.com or upon request from the Reader Service.

We make a portion of our mailing list available to reputable third parties that offer products we believe may interest you. If you prefer that we not exchange your name with third parties, or if you wish to clarify or modify your communication preferences, please visit us at www.ReaderService.com/consumerschoice or write to us at Reader Service Preference Service, P.O. Box 9062, Buffalo, NY 14269. Include your complete name and address.

LIREG11

With time running out to stop the Lions of Texas from orchestrating their evil plan, Texas Ranger Levi McDonall must work with his childhood friend to solve his captain's murder and thwart the group's disastrous plot. Read on for a preview of OUT OF TIME by Shirlee McCoy, the exciting conclusion to the TEXAS RANGER JUSTICE *series.*

Silence told its own story, and Susannah Jorgenson listened as she hurried across the bridge that led to the Alamo Chapel. Darkness had fallen hours ago and the air held a hint of rain. The shadows seemed deeper than usual, the darkness just a little blacker. Or maybe it was simply her imagination that made the Alamo complex seem so forbidding.

She shivered. Not from the cold. Not from the chilly breeze. From the darkness, the silence, the endless echo of her fear as she made her final rounds. She jogged to the chapel and flashed the beam of her light along the corners of the building.

Nothing.

No movement, no sounds, no reason to think she wasn't alone, but she couldn't shake the feeling that she was being watched. That somewhere beyond the beam of her light, danger waited. She did a full sweep of the chapel and of the office area beyond. Nothing, of course.

She opened the chapel door, stepping straight into a broad, muscular chest. Someone grabbed her upper arms, holding her in place.

She shoved forward into her attacker, pushing her weight into a solid wall of strength as she tried to unbalance him.

"Calm down. I was just trying to keep you from falling." The man released his hold.

"Sorry about that. I wasn't expecting anyone to be standing near the door. We're closed for the day, but we'll be open again at seven tomorrow morning." She cleared her throat.

"No need to apologize. I'm Ranger Levi McDonall. My captain said he was going to call and let you know I was on the way."

"Levi McDonall?" Her childhood idol? Her best guy friend? Her first teenage crush?

No way could they be the same.

"Come on in." She hurried into the chapel, trying to pull herself together. This was the Texas Ranger she'd be working with for the next eight days?

She flipped on a light, turned to face McDonall.

Levi McDonall.

Her Levi McDonall.

Can Levi and Susannah put the past behind them to save San Antonio's future? Find out in OUT OF TIME by Shirlee McCoy from Love Inspired Suspense, available in June wherever books are sold.

SHLISEXP0611